SARAH'S LIST

DENICE HOLT

Copyright © 2022 by Denice Holt

All rights reserved.

No part of this book may be reproduced in any form or by any electronic or mechanical means, including information storage and retrieval systems, without written permission from the author, except for the use of brief quotations in a book review.

Copyright © 2022 by Denice Holt

All rights reserved.

This is a work of fiction. Unless otherwise indicated, all the names, characters, businesses, places, events and incidents in this book are either the product of the author's imagination or used in a fictitious manner. Any resemblance to actual persons, living or dead, or actual events is purely coincidental.

Published in 2022 by FCM Publishing

(ebook) ISBN: 978-1-957047-06-5

(paperback) ISBN: 978-1-957047-07-2

CHAPTER ONE

"We didn't order these," Sarah said as their server placed two shots on the table.

"They're from the young men at the bar," the server replied, nodding to a couple of well-dressed men, each wearing an expensive suit and a smile.

"Well, that was thoughtful," Monica said, reaching for a glass. "What are they?"

"Lemon drops," the server said.

Sarah turned to see who was funding this round of syrupy trouble. "Aren't they a little young to be out this late on a school night?" she asked.

"Shut up, Sarah," Monica said, toasting her glass in the boys' direction. "Besides, it's Friday."

Sarah lifted her glass, not bothering to turn around. In unison, she and Monica threw back their shots.

Monica let a slow moan of enjoyment slip out as she licked the sweet lemon flavor off of her lips. "Mmmm."

"I didn't realize you were such a big fan of lemon drops," Sarah said.

"Honestly, I'm not," Monica said, waving the server back to the table. "I just like doing shots."

Sarah groaned. "Oh Lord, please don't start this again."

"One's not going to kill you."

The server quickly made his way back to the table. "How can I help you, ladies?"

"What is your best tequila?" Monica inquired.

"Ma'am, we have a broad selection of tequila in taste and cost, so it's hard for me to say which is the best."

"If money weren't an issue, which would you drink?" Monica asked.

The server pondered for a second. "If money is no issue? For me, Don Julio REAL."

"Fine. Then I want four shots of that. Two for us and two for the gentlemen at the bar," she said as she poked Sarah in the side.

"What are you doing?" Sarah asked, not bothering to conceal the depth of her annoyance.

Monica shook her head as she slurped the last of her vodka on the rocks through a straw. "Have you been married so long that you don't remember what it's like to flirt with a man?"

"It hasn't occurred to me to flirt with anyone since the day Jack and I married," Sarah replied.

Monica returned her attention to her empty drink, sucking air through her straw for an obnoxiously long time.

"Do you want me to order you another drink?" Sarah asked, annoyed by the spectacle Monica was making.

"I believe I just did," Monica replied with a smile. She nodded at the bar, "Don't you miss flirting? I mean, it's the best part of foreplay."

"I flirt with Jack."

"That's different."

"How's it different?" Sarah asked.

"It's different because you know with Jack, it automatically ends with sex. With someone you've just met, it's yet to be determined, and I think that's much more exciting."

Sarah quietly took a sip of her wine.

"You disagree?" Monica inquired.

Sarah shrugged her shoulders.

"What's the matter with you?" Monica asked.

"Sex isn't as automatic with Jack as you might think," Sarah said, not looking up from her glass.

"Whoa," Monica said, turning back to Sarah. "Trouble in paradise?"

Sarah sat quietly without saying anything.

"Sarah, I'm your best friend. You can't say something like that without elaborating."

"We're fine."

"Doesn't sound fine to me at all."

"I don't know why I said that. Everything is fine."

Monica sat for a moment, trying to wrap her head around this information. "Sarah, you just said that sex with Jack isn't 'automatic' and that it's just 'fine.' What I hear you saying is that you aren't having sex with your husband and that you're okay with it."

"We have sex," Sarah said quickly.

"Really?"

"Really."

"When was the last time you two made love? And be honest," Monica pressed.

"I don't know," Sarah replied, sorry that she had opened the door for this conversation. "Maybe a couple of weeks ago."

"My God, Sarah. Maybe a couple of weeks ago?" Staring at her in disbelief, Monica added, "Does that mean that it could possibly, actually, maybe be three weeks? Or maybe four weeks?"

Sarah took a sip of her wine without making eye contact with Monica. "Maybe."

During the awkward silence that followed, the server walked up and placed shots on the table in front of them along with another vodka for Monica.

"Thank you very much, garçon," Monica said. "Now, if you would be a dear and start preparing Round Two? We are definitely going to need a Round Two."

"Shots for the gentlemen as well?" the server asked.

"Of course," Monica said.

As the server walked away, Sarah gave Monica a dirty look. "That doesn't mean what you think it does."

"What?"

"Garçon."

"It means waiter in French," Monica said.

"No, it doesn't. It means boy in French," Sarah said.

"I don't think it does, but we can agree to disagree." Lifting her shot glass in the air, she said, "To finding your way back to great sex." Then, under her breath, she added, "Assuming it was ever great."

Sarah didn't have the energy to argue. After lifting her glass towards the gentlemen at the bar, she clinked glasses with Monica and shot the tequila.

"Oh, damn, that's trouble," Sarah said.

"Holy cow, yes, it is," Monica confirmed. "Hey boy," Monica yelled at their server. "Hurry up with the next round!"

Sarah rolled her eyes.

"So let me ask you this," Monica said, returning their conversation to Sarah's sex life. "When was the last time you masturbated?"

"Monica, that's none of your business," Sarah said, looking at her in disbelief.

"Well, I assume you do masturbate?"

Sarah held her empty wine glass up in the direction of the server and pointed at it. "We are not having this conversation," she said.

"You're being childish, Sarah. I'm a woman. I masturbate. I've been married. Twice. I know the trials and tribulations of married sex. I promise I've been there before."

"I doubt that," Sarah said quietly.

"Listen, it is far better that you tell me than have my imagination fill in the blanks."

Sarah didn't reply.

"Jack has a small dick," Monica said, confirming the dangers of having her imagination fill in the blanks.

"His dick is adequate."

"Adequate means small."

"No, it doesn't. It gets the job done, and that's all I need. Good enough is perfect," Sarah said.

"Using that logic, Sarah, digging a hole with a soup spoon is just as good as using a shovel," Monica said, not intending to come across as bitchy as it sounded. "I mean, you could do it, but why would you want to?"

"You're unbelievable," Sarah said, looking for the server.

When the next round of drinks appeared, Sarah grabbed a shot off the tray before he had time to come to a complete stop. She slammed it without waiting on Monica or the boys.

"This afternoon," Sarah said, wiping tequila off her mouth with her sleeve and grabbing the glass of wine off the tray.

"What about it?" Monica asked.

"That was the last time I masturbated."

The server's eyes went wide as he slowly tried to disappear into the ether.

"Now we're getting somewhere," Monica said with a smile.

"Are we really going to have this conversation?" Sarah asked.

"Absolutely," Monica said.

Sarah leaned across the table, grabbed Monica's tequila, and drank it before Monica could say a word. "Then you might want to keep these coming."

Monica looked back at their waiter and waved her hand through the air in a big circle, giving the universal sign for another round. Returning her attention to Sarah, she continued. "So, this afternoon, before you picked Colin up from school?"

"Actually..." Sarah said, leaving her sentence unfinished.

"Actually, what?"

"I did it where I almost always do it...two or three times a week...Monday through Friday."

Monica scooted forward in her seat and leaned in closer. "Oh my, do tell."

Sarah sat there playing with her wine glass, biting her lower lip.

"Tell me, Sarah!"

Sarah looked up with a sheepish smile. "In the carpool lane at Colin's school."

Monica leaned back and looked at Sarah with a huge grin.

"It's gross, I know," Sarah said. "It sounds even worse when I say it out loud. I was disgusted with myself before, but now...."

Monica leaned across the table and held her hands. "Sarah, there is nothing gross about it. If I told you about some of the times, places, and people in my life? I could show you gross. You aren't even scratching the surface."

"I doubt that," Sarah said.

"If you don't mind me asking," Monica said, with a mischievous smile, "what do you fantasize about when you masturbate?"

Before Sarah could answer, she realized that the two men

from the bar had just walked up. Sarah glared at Monica and slumped low in her seat.

"We wanted to deliver this round of shots personally to thank you properly, but please, ladies...we don't want to interrupt," one of the young men said with a grin. "Continue. Where were you? Ah, yes, what do you fantasize about when you masturbate?"

"Hello, boys," Monica said, winking at Sarah.

"Before you answer," the young man continued, "I want to offer my full support for any fantasies involving smoking-hot cougars picking up young professional men in a bar."

Sarah looked at the young man as he passed the glasses out to everyone at the table. He was classically handsome, well built, and carried himself with more confidence than anyone in his early twenties should have. Sarah had a regular fantasy about a young man like this, and the last thing she needed to be doing was drinking shots of tequila with a living, breathing, warm-blooded version of him.

The young man smiled as he looked around the group, looking at Sarah last. Holding eye contact with her, he offered a toast. "May your life be filled with fantasies...And a partner willing to make them all come true."

CHAPTER TWO

"Hey, Jack," the voice said through the phone.

"Monica?" Jack asked. "Is everything okay?"

"Yeah, well, we'll be pulling up in a sec. I'm going to need some help," Monica said, her words slurring as she started to giggle.

"Is Sarah okay?" he asked.

"I'm not going to lie, Jack. It's not pretty."

"Monica, is Sarah okay?" he demanded.

"Well, she will be. Just meet me outside, okay?" Monica said as she hung up the phone.

Jack walked out on his front porch just in time to see the limo pull to a stop. The rear door flew open, and his wife threw up in the street next to the curb.

Monica stumbled out of the opposite side of the limo. "Don't worry, Jack. She left most of her dinner back on the Bruckner Expressway. At this point, I'm sure she's just down to water and stomach acid," Monica said, loud enough for the world to hear.

"Monica, stop yelling. I don't need my neighbors listening to this."

"Screw your rich, stuffy neighbors, Jack," she replied.

The chauffeur quickly walked back to greet Jack. "I'm so sorry, Mr. Williams. By the time I realized there was a problem, it was too late," he said in a thick Russian accent.

"No worries, Yuri. You don't get paid to babysit."

"Yes, but..."

"Yuri, it's not your fault. I don't blame you for this," Jack said, glaring at Monica.

"Don't look at me like that, Jack. Sarah did this all on her own," Monica said.

Jack carefully reached into the limo and lifted a curl of her brunette hair out of her face and placed it back over her shoulder. "Babe, are you okay?"

"Hi, Jack," Sarah slurred.

"Honey, can you walk?"

"I'm okay."

"Can you walk?" he asked again.

"Can I walk?" Sarah asked, looking up at him, perplexed. "Of course I can walk." With that, she took one step out of the limo and fell to her knees. "Ooops." She giggled. "What do you know? I can't walk."

Jack bent down and lifted her in his arms. "My God, you smell like tequila and vomit."

"I ordered the tequila. I didn't order any vomit," she said, wiping her mouth with her sleeve.

Yuri quickly leaned in to take Sarah from Jack. "Allow me to help," he said.

"I've got her, Yuri. Thanks. Please, just get Monica home safely."

"Are you sure?"

"Yes, I'm sure. Thanks."

Yuri slowly returned to the driver's side door, watching Jack the whole way before climbing back into the limo.

While Jack carried Sarah up the stairs to the front door, her shoe fell off into a bush. "My shoe!" she yelled, dragging the word shoe out like she was singing.

Jack continued to walk.

"My shoe, Jack. I lost my shoe."

"Babe, I will come back and get your shoe," he said with growing frustration.

"I can't lose that shoe, Jack. It's my favorite."

"They're all your favorite."

"No, but these really are my favorite," she pleaded.

"I will get your shoe," he repeated.

Pausing at the front door, he turned to face Monica. "What the hell happened? How did your girls' night turn into a frat party?"

"Well, you should think more bachelorette party...though, to be honest, there were a couple of rather cute young men there."

"Excuse me?" Jack asked.

"Not my story to tell, big guy. You're going to have to ask her." With that, Monica got in the limo and slammed the door.

Jack stood there for a moment in disbelief. He started to ask Sarah what the hell Monica was talking about, but Sarah was softly talking to herself in her sleep on his shoulder. Stepping inside, Jack closed the door and carefully made his way to their bedroom. Just as he was about to lay her on the bed, Sarah started to cough as if she would throw up again. Jack got her to the bathroom just in time for dry heaves to begin. He pulled her hair back over her shoulders and grabbed a cold, wet facecloth.

"I'm going to go grab some water. I'll be right back."

"Okay, I'll wait right here," she said.

Jack ran down to the kitchen and returned with a bottle of water and a glass of ginger ale over ice. He sat down beside her and held the water up to her lips. Coughing up half the water she swallowed, he took the washcloth and wiped her mouth. Sarah took another sip before laying her head down on her arm that spanned the toilet.

"You're the best husband ever."

He gently rubbed her hair.

"In fact, you are the perfect husband."

"Okay, babe, let me know when you think you can make it to the bed."

"I just need two minutes."

"Okay."

"Where was I?" she said to herself. "Oh yeah, best everything. Best prep school. Best college. Best job on Wall Street."

"Okay, babe."

"You have it all," she said, ending with a burp. "We have it all."

Jack continued to rub her hair.

"Two point three kids and a white picket fence," she said as if she was yelling to someone in the next room.

Jack stood up and tried to give her a hand. "Okay, Sarah, let's go to bed, please?"

"I just need two more minutes. Just two."

Jack sat back down and returned to rubbing her hair.

"I have a perfectly adequate sex life with my husband's perfectly adequate penis."

"Excuse me?" Jack replied. But no sooner did the words leave his mouth than Sarah's dry heaves returned.

After a minute, she composed herself and continued. "Everything is perfect."

Jack wiped her mouth with a cool, wet facecloth and held some ginger ale up for her to sip.

"Mmmm...ginger ale," she said, taking another sip. "Because it's perfect and you're perfect." She put her head down on her arm again and closed her eyes. "You know, Jack, you don't want me anymore."

"You're being silly. You know I want you."

"Not like you used to," she said. "I think ever since you saw my vagina spit out a human being, you've changed."

"That's nonsense."

"No. It's not," she said sternly. "It used to be your fun box, and now all you see is a baby-making machine."

"Okay, that's enough."

"But then again, you always wanted to try anal, and you don't want that anymore, either."

Jack tried to lift her.

"No, two minutes. Just give me two more minutes." She reached her free arm around his leg trying to keep him from leaving. "There were boys at the bar tonight who wanted me. They really wanted me. It reminded me of you when you wanted me."

"Sarah, you're drunk. Can we go to bed, please?"

"I have a secret," Sarah drunk whispered even though nobody else was around to listen. "Do you want to know my secret?"

Jack didn't say anything.

"I masturbate in the school carpool lane. A lot, Jack. And you want to know why? Because it feels wrong. And I love it. People are looking at me and, in my mind, I pretend they know exactly what I'm doing."

The revelation left Jack in shock.

"I even have a special little vibrator I keep in my purse just for the school carpool lane. It's my school carpool lane vibrator." She lifted her head as if she was about to throw up again, but after a moment, she laid her head back down on her arm.

"It looks just like Chapstick. But it's not Chapstick. It's way better than Chapstick."

Jack's head was spinning. He felt like he was reading her diary, but he couldn't bring himself to stop her.

"And do you know what I fantasize about when I sit in the school carpool lane, Jack...do you want to know?

Jack said nothing

"Do you want to know? I'll tell you if you want to know... but you have to ask."

Jack was afraid to ask. But he had to know.

"I want to know."

"You have to say please."

"Will you please tell me what you fantasize about?"

"Yes, Jack. I will tell you."

Over the next twenty minutes, Sarah listed out almost a dozen recurring fantasies she would masturbate to while waiting to pick her son up from school. By the time Jack tucked her into bed, he had realized that he didn't know his wife as well as he thought. He tossed and turned next to her, trying to sleep. But thoughts raced through his head. Jack wasn't a control freak, but he didn't like being out of control, either. With this information, he was at a total loss. And that was not a feeling he liked at all.

CHAPTER THREE

"Good morning, Mommy."

How could such a small voice cause so much pain?

Forcing her eyes open, Sarah saw her four-year-old son at the side of the bed, trying to climb in with her.

"Colin, I told you to let Mommy sleep," Jack said, following on his son's heels into the bedroom. "Now get back downstairs."

"Are you feeling better, Mommy?" Colin asked.

Jack swooped him up in his arms. "Yes, buddy. Mommy will feel better soon."

"Daddy's making pancakes. Maybe pancakes would make you feel better," Colin suggested.

Jack set him down outside their bedroom and gave him a little pat on the rear. "I'll be down in a second." Looking back at Sarah, he said, "Sorry. I tried to let you sleep."

"Jack?" Sarah asked in barely a whisper.

"Yeah?"

"What the hell happened last night?"

Jack couldn't help but laugh. "You're asking me?"

She was rubbing her temples with her eyes closed, desperately trying to piece together anything about the evening. "I vaguely remember going to a bar after dinner. But I have nothing after that."

"Maybe you got roofied," Jack said.

"I didn't get roofied."

"Maybe you roofied yourself with shots of tequila?" Jack suggested playfully.

With that news, she let out a long groan. "Monica and the damn tequila."

"Every time, babe. Every time."

"We are definitely not friends," Sarah said in a pained voice.

"Who? You and Monica or you and tequila?"

Sarah rolled over and put her head under a pillow. "At the moment, I don't like either one."

"Well, I've never much liked Monica, so...."

"Jack, please," she said, finally opening her eyes. "How did I get home?"

"Yuri."

"I don't remember that at all."

"You don't remember throwing up on the Bruckner?"

"Oh god."

"How about the young men at the bar who wanted to have sex with you?"

She immediately pulled the pillow off her face. "That's not true. Did Monica tell you that?" Sarah asked, looking at the ceiling.

"No," Jack said. "You did."

Sarah sat straight up in bed. "Oh, please tell me you're kidding?"

"And what about the school carpool lane? Do you remember that discussion?" Jack asked, waiting to see the facial expression when that news landed.

Sarah laid back down and pulled the pillow over her face.

And started to cry. Jack waited a second before crawling up on the bed beside her and lifting the pillow.

"Hey," he said. "Hey, it's okay."

"Jack..."

"Sarah, it's going to be fine."

"Going to be? I don't even know what to say right now. I don't think I've ever been this embarrassed in my life."

Jack wiped the tears off her cheek and leaned in to kiss her. "I promise it's going to be fine."

"Seriously, can we agree right now never to discuss this again? Please?"

Jack smiled down at her. "Oh, we have a lot to discuss, Mrs. Williams. Starting with your perfectly adequate sex life with your husband's perfectly adequate penis."

Sarah groaned again, rolled over, and buried her head in the covers. "Just shoot me. Please, just get it over with and shoot me."

He hopped out of bed and headed for the door. "You better get up and moving before your mother sees you like this."

She quickly rolled over and sat up in bed. "My mother?"

"Yes. Your mother. She's coming to spend the night with Colin."

"And why do we need her to do that?"

"Because, my dear wife, you and I are going on a date. We have lots to discuss." With that, he disappeared downstairs.

Sarah laid back down and returned her gaze to the ceiling. She was terrified at the prospect of what she might have told him. If she confessed to the carpool lane activities, what else did she say? The one thing that gave her hope was that he had kissed her and said everything would be okay. Had she told him everything, he would have already packed his bags.

She got out of bed and made her way to the bathroom. Dumping a liberal amount of lavender essential oil in a hot bath, she gently lowered herself down into the water. Moments later, Jack appeared with a Bloody Mary in hand. He leaned in for a kiss as he handed it to her.

"Really?" is all she could say.

"Hair-of-the-dog is a terrible lifetime strategy. But for today? I believe it's just what the doctor ordered."

Sarah took a sip. "That's perfect. Thanks."

Jack looked down and smiled. "Well, I am the perfect husband, after all," he said with a giant grin.

Sarah looked up at him. "You are the perfect husband, but I'm not sure why that's funny."

"In due time, Sarah. In due time," he said as he turned to leave.

"Hey, Jack?" she asked.

He stopped at the bathroom door and turned around. "What's up?"

"Are we good? You and me?"

Jack thought about it for a second before replying. "Yeah, I think we will be," he said with a wink.

Sarah took one more sip of her drink and placed it beside the tub. Slowly slipping her entire body underwater, she felt much better about things. A kiss. A wink. A Bloody Mary. There's no way she shared her fantasies with him. No way.

CHAPTER FOUR

Sarah stood in the bathroom. "If you don't tell me what we're doing, I'll have no idea what to pack."

"Just pack your normal bathroom stuff," Jack said.

"I don't need to pack any clothes?"

"No."

Jack told Sarah that they would be spending the night out and nothing more. There was an element to the not knowing that excited Sarah, but her OCD was kicking in. "You have to give me some idea of what we're doing."

Jack smiled as he walked out of the closet with a garment bag. "You'll be fine, I promise."

"Wait, that isn't fair. You're bringing clothes?"

"Trust me. You'll be fine."

Though she wanted to press, she decided she was pushing her luck already. Sarah packed everything she could think of that she might need from the bathroom. Then, when Jack wasn't looking, she threw a change of clothes into an overnight bag.

As she came down the stairs, she could see her mom pulling up in front of the house. "Colin, Granna is here."

Colin came racing out of the kitchen and straight to the front door. "Granna!"

Sarah opened the door just in time for her son to skirt by her and wrap his arms around his grandmother.

"I missed you, Granna," he said, though it hadn't been more than a few days since he saw her last.

"I missed you, too, dear," she replied.

Pointing to the red object in her hand, Colin asked, "Is that for me?"

"No, dear, that's a shoe I found outside in a bush," she said. "Sarah, why is there a shoe in your bush?"

Sarah did a double-take with Jack as if to say what-the-hell. He just smiled and shrugged his shoulders. Turning back to her mother, she said, "Mom, I can honestly say I have no idea."

"Hello, Maureen," Jack said as he leaned over and kissed his mother-in-law on the cheek. "Thanks for coming on such short notice."

"Well, Jack, it isn't a good business practice to spring an overnight obligation on employees. I hope you tell your boss that it isn't reasonable to expect you to drop everything last minute."

"That's why they pay him the big bucks, Mom," Sarah said quickly.

"Jack," Maureen said, holding the shoe out to him. "Do you know why there is a shoe in your bush?"

Jack smiled. "Maureen, I think it's a new game the kids are playing these days. The Johnson's had one in their bush last week. I don't really see the humor in it, but you can just throw it in the garbage," he said, trying not to make eye contact with Sarah.

"Here, Mom, let me take that," Sarah said, grabbing the shoe and scowling at Jack.

She quickly ran upstairs to place it back where it belonged. She would try to remember to ask how it got there.

"Babe, the car is here," Jack yelled upstairs.

"Coming," she replied.

Jack gave Colin a big hug. "Be good for Granna, please?"

"I will," he said.

Sarah came down the stairs with two bags in her hand, which earned her a dirty look from Jack. "Goodbye, Mom. Thanks again," she said.

"Anytime, dear."

"Colin, you be good. I love you!" she said as she lifted him off the ground.

"I love you, Mommy," he said as he kissed her goodbye.

Sarah handed Colin to her mother and headed out the door.

By the time she got to the limo, Jack had already opened some champagne. Yuri took the bags from Sarah, placed them in the trunk, and returned to help her into the limo.

As Sarah took a seat beside Jack, he held up a glass for her and smiled.

"What are you up to, mister?" Sarah said, suspicious of everything going on.

"You're on a need-to-know basis," he said with a grin. "And you don't need to know."

"Does Yuri know where we're going?" she asked sarcastically.

"Of course, he does. He needed to know."

They clinked their glasses, and each had a sip. "I'm not sure this is the best way to reward bad behavior," Sarah said as she leaned over against his side.

"Well, I have to take responsibility for some of this."

"How so?" she asked.

"It shouldn't have taken you getting blackout drunk to share your...desires...with me."

Sarah sat up quickly. "What do you mean 'share my desires'?"

Jack looked surprised. "I told you we discussed what you fantasize about when you masturbate."

A look of terror flew across her face. "No, Jack, you didn't tell me that."

"Yes, I did."

"You told me that I confessed to masturbating in the carpool lane. You didn't say anything about sharing fantasies."

Jack laughed to himself. "Oh, sorry. I thought I did."

Sarah sat there for a moment, trying to compose herself. "What exactly did I tell you?"

"God, Sarah, I have to be honest. I hope you told me all of them," he said as he sipped champagne. "Because, if there are more, I honestly can't imagine what they might be."

"Which fantasies?" she asked, borderline pleading.

"Sex in public."

"Okay."

"Being blindfolded and tied to a bed and having a stranger go down on you."

"Oh lord."

"Having intercourse with a stranger."

"Enough."

"Having sex with a BBC."

"Okay. Stop."

Sarah brought her hand in front of her mouth and turned to look out the window. "I am so sorry. You know those are just fantasies, right?"

He reached out and took her hand. "Listen, I've never shot for 'adequate' at anything in my life. You telling me that our sex life was 'perfectly adequate' cut me to the core. The notion that the time you spend with me is adequate and the time you spend with your vibrator is exciting is just salt in the wound."

"Jack, it's fantasy," she stressed to him.

"I don't care what it is. If that is what you think about, that's what you deserve."

"It's just fantasy," Sarah pleaded.

"Yeah, so far. But that doesn't mean fantasies can't come true."

Sarah leaned over, took his glass, and placed it along with hers in a holder on the side of the limo. She turned to face him and took his hands in hers. "Listen, I understand how what I said could be construed as bad, but you should hear my friends complain. They would kill for a sex life that they could describe as adequate."

Jack sat for a second before picking up his drink and taking a sip. "I'm not sure how to say this, so I'm just going to say it. You let the genie out of the bottle. And no road gets it back in. What I'm proposing here is the only way I see that we get to a place in our relationship where we can both be happy."

"Crap, what does that even mean?"

"You'll know when you need to know."

"Jack?"

"Sarah?"

She grabbed her champagne and tipped it back until it was gone. "Jack Williams, against my better judgment, I will go along with whatever this is."

"Thank you."

"You better not fuck this up."

CHAPTER FIVE

After checking into the brand-new Aspect East Village Hotel, now the tallest hotel in lower Manhattan, they walked down to a small Italian restaurant on Twenty-Fourth and Park. Jack was about to pay the bill when he suggested that Sarah finish her meal.

"This might be the last real food you get today," he said.

"What does that mean?" Sarah asked, taking a sip of Chianti.

"I'm just saying we don't have any dinner plans tonight. And I'm not sure what the food options will be."

Sarah looked across the table and let out a giant exhale. "Okay, mystery man, whatever you say. I'm just along for the ride. Now, let me ask you this. This meal was good, but we passed a lot of excellent restaurants along the way to get here."

"We didn't come to this part of town for the food; you are correct," he said as he signed the credit card slip. "Come on."

Sarah stood up, took his hand, and followed by his side. Jack didn't break stride as he walked straight across the street, almost getting them run over by a cab.

"Hey, where are we going that's worth getting us killed?"

"Right here," he said, pointing to the door with a small sign, "Looks of NY."

"And what exactly is this?"

"Trust, remember?" he asked with a grin.

"Lead on," she said, resigned to her fate.

Once they were through the door, Sarah heard it lock behind them. Jack looked up and gave a brief wave to the video camera in the corner of the ceiling. A moment later, there was a loud electronic buzz, and the inner door opened. Jack turned to Sarah and raised his eyebrows, excited like a child on Christmas morning.

It immediately became clear to Sarah that they were in a high-end sex shop. The store had everything from delicate lingerie to elegant see-through gowns to a whole room dedicated to pain and bondage. Sarah swung around on the spot and headed back towards the door. Jack grabbed her arm, spun her around, and wrapped her up in his arms.

"First time, huh?" asked the cute, tattoo-covered, size two from behind the counter.

"That obvious?" Jack asked.

"Where are you going?" Size Two asked.

Sarah looked at Jack. Jack just shrugged his shoulders.

"Ok, let me guess: Kitties? Velvet?" She waited a second. "No, you are definitely Lux people."

Jack smiled. "You are correct."

"Knew it," Size Two said.

Sarah did a double-take between her husband and Size Two. "Does anyone want to repeat that, but in English this time?"

Size Two looked at Jack. "You didn't tell her?"

"No. Not yet."

"Well, that's one way to go," she said. "You looking for something for her to wear?"

"Yup," Jack said.

Walking from behind the counter, she said, "I'm Brooke. Come with me."

Sarah gave Jack a dirty look.

"Hurry," Jack said. "Catch up."

Sarah shook her head and fell in step behind Brooke. They walked through a series of rooms, including one with a frightening display of dildos, before entering a room with nothing but clothes. Brooke looked through several clothes racks, selected three skimpy dresses, then handed them to Sarah.

"I'll never get into a four," Sarah protested.

"Trust me. These will fit you how he wants them to fit," Brooke said.

"How *he* wants them to fit?"

"Just try them on, and don't overthink it," Brooke said.

Sarah held them up for Jack to see and rolled her eyes. "Where the hell do you think you're taking me wearing something like this?"

Jack smiled. "Hey, come on. You heard the woman. Don't overthink it," he said with a grin.

"Geronimo it," Brooke said.

"Geronimo?"

"Yeah, it means to throw caution to the wind and just jump in."

"Super," Sarah said.

"I think it started with people parachuting out of airplanes," Brooke added.

"So, you're saying I am about to jump off of something?"

"Well, jump off or jump in. Either way, it will be exciting," Brooke said.

She walked up behind Sarah and handed her a pair of shoes. "Six and a half? These will look great with any of those," she said.

Sarah apprehensively accepted the shoes and disappeared back into the dressing room. A moment later, she called out to Jack. "I'm not coming out wearing this," she said.

"Geronimo, baby," Jack yelled back.

"Geronimo, my ass," she yelled in reply.

Jack looked to Brooke for some assistance. Brooke just smiled and nodded.

"Sarah, try all of them on, and then pick your favorite and let us see that one."

They could hear a groan come from the dressing room. A few minutes later, Sarah came out in a sexy, low-cut, green dress that hugged her curves beautifully. With an arm across her chest and a hand covering between her legs, Sarah shuffled in front of a full-length mirror.

"Holy cow," Jack said.

"I'd say," Brooke added.

"I look completely ridiculous," Sarah said, looking in the mirror.

"You look totally hot," Brooke said. "It's perfect for Lux. I mean, as long as you don't actually wear a bra and underwear with it."

Sarah immediately glared at her husband. "Jack?"

"But the other women will hate you," Brooke added.

Jack walked around her, looking from all angles. "Sarah, what's the matter with this? You look amazing."

"This isn't me. I don't dress like this."

Jack walked up and spun her around in front of the mirror. "Just look at you."

"I'm sorry, Jack. It just isn't me."

Jack thought for a second and then took a seat on the bench next to Brooke. "Do you know who would never wear that?" Jack asked.

"Most people," Sarah replied.

"My wife or my kid's mom."

"Yeah, that's what I've been trying to tell you."

"Well, I should have made myself clear. I'm not taking my wife out tonight. And I sure as hell am not bringing my kid's mom to Lux."

"Oh really. And who exactly did you plan on going with?" Sarah inquired sarcastically.

"My girlfriend or maybe just a lover. I'll let you pick."

"You tell her, Jack," Brooke said.

Sarah walked over and shooed Brooke away. "Okay, Brooke, that's enough help for one day. Please let me speak with my husband alone."

"That's fine and all. I'm just saying you are one hot momma in that outfit," she said before walking back to the front of the store.

Sarah walked over and sat on the bench. She gently leaned her head against Jack's shoulder. "Will you be honest with me? Why did you bring me here?"

Jack rubbed her leg for a bit before answering. "Sarah. I didn't bring us here. You did. If you were satisfied with adequate, we'd be home sitting on the couch watching TV."

Sarah took his hand in hers. "This scares me to death."

"Well, it scares me, too."

"Then why are we doing it?"

"Because a lifetime of adequate scares me more."

Sarah stood up. "Okay, I'll do this. But I can say without question that after a lifetime of 'adequate' with the man I married, I would still love you. When we get through with whatever this is that you are up to, I hope that I feel the same way."

She disappeared into the back. Jack knew that he was playing with fire, but he had told her the truth. He was more afraid of living a lifetime of adequate. Chips fall where they may; there was no turning back now.

CHAPTER SIX

Brooke had a few parting thoughts for them as they left the store. She suggested that they buy a long coat for Sarah because she probably didn't want to wear that dress "in public, public." She also reminded Jack that Lux didn't have a liquor license, so he needed to bring whatever they planned on drinking. And finally, she said that Sarah's outfit would not be complete without a long strand of pearls. "And I know you have the money, Jack. I can smell Wall Street on you from a mile away."

Jack did as he was told.

Back at the hotel, Sarah and Jack had more fun simply getting ready for the evening than they had had in a long time. Playing music, laughing, drinking, a spontaneous pillow fight. Sarah wasn't sure where they went from there, but it was an excellent start to the evening.

Pulling up in front of an ordinary-looking apartment building, Sarah grabbed Jack's hand as he began to climb out. "Okay, enough. Whose apartment is this?"

"It's not an apartment. It's a club. Now come on," he said, stepping out of the limo.

"A club?" Sarah asked as she followed him out onto the sidewalk.

"A club," he repeated. Once the limo had pulled away from the curb, he added, "A sex club."

Sarah stopped in her tracks. She started to say something, but the look on Jack's face made her think better of it. Instead, she just squeezed his hand and stepped towards the door.

The interior of the building looked like a luxury hotel. A large well-dressed man greeted them at the door and guided them off to a side counter designated for member services. Gesturing at the beautiful, scantily dressed woman behind the counter, he said, "Tiffany will take care of you."

"Welcome," she said, looking down from behind the counter. "May I see your IDs?"

"Hi, Jack and Sarah Williams," Jack said, reaching for his driver's license.

Tiffany smiled. "Jack, while they are at the club, most members choose not to verbalize their full name. I need a copy of a photo ID on file for security purposes, but other than that, you are welcome to remain on a first name or social name basis."

"Social name?" Jack asked.

"It's a polite way of saying a fake name."

"Ah," he said.

"I will give you a member number, and you will use it for accessing your lockers and storing your alcohol. Now, I'll need you both to read through this waiver and sign, please," she said as she handed over two iPads.

Sitting beside each other on a bench, Sarah began to read sections of the waiver out loud in borderline disbelief.

"I am not offended by public nudity? I am not offended by public sex?" She laid the iPad on her lap and looked over at Jack. "Are you kidding me?"

Jack laughed, "That's nothing. Wait until you get to number twelve."

"I am not offended by the sight of bodily fluids? Jack, tell me this is a joke?"

"Geronimo, baby. Just sign it, and let's go."

Sarah rapidly checked through everything on the list, and with a deep exhale, she signed the bottom. "Okay. I hope you know what you're doing."

It took about five minutes for Tiffany to get everything squared away in the computer, and then she stepped down and led them to large double doors behind the counter. "Let me give you a quick tour."

After the waiver, Sarah was terrified to see what awaited them on the other side of the doors, but she was surprised. It simply looked like a high-end nightclub. Granted, most women were wearing outfits you wouldn't see in a typical nightclub, as she would be once she removed her coat, but there was no sex or bodily fluids to be seen. There was a large dancefloor in the middle of the room filled with couples. And a bar wrapped around the outside wall staffed with several attractive bartenders. Finally, off to one side, there was an elaborate dinner buffet. Tiffany took their bottle of vodka, placed a sticker on it with their member number, and handed it back to one of the bartenders.

"The bartenders are excellent," she said. "It won't take them long to memorize your member number. Until then, remind them of it whenever you want a drink. They should have any mixer you can think of back there."

Sarah loved to dance, and the music they were playing was some of her favorite. Though the skimpy dress she was wearing still made her a little nervous, she was beginning to relax and enjoy the evening.

"Come this way," Tiffany said. "And I'll show you the back rooms."

Sarah immediately clenched Jack's arm. "Back rooms?"

"It's okay, babe. You're going to be fine," Jack reassured her.

Walking through another set of doors, Tiffany added, "Normally, people aren't allowed back here with clothes on, but we make an exception for the tours."

"Wait," Sarah said. "You have to be naked?"

Tiffany gave a knowing smirk to Jack before qualifying. "No, you can wear lingerie or just wrap yourself up in a towel if you don't want to be nude."

"Fuck me, Jack. The next time you ask me to jump off something, how about telling me how far I have to fall?"

"Just wait," Tiffany said with a smile, leading them further into the back rooms. "Here are the locker rooms where you can store your things. Just let the attendant know your member number, and she will open your locker for you."

"Is this the men's locker room or the women's locker room?" Sarah asked.

"Good one," Tiffany said, walking them through to the other side. "Bathrooms on this side, showers on this side, and through here is the back."

Jack saw a funny look on Sarah's face as they approached the next set of doors. It took him a second to realize that she was staring at an enormous glass bowl filled with condoms.

"Sarah, I promise you're going to be okay. I promise," Jack said once again.

Tiffany stopped and took Sarah's hands, and looked her in the eyes. "Sarah, everyone is here to have a good time. But what that means to one is not what it means to everyone. Half the people are here to have sex in front of others or watch people have sex in front of them. If you two want to find another couple or a single man or a single woman to play with, that will be available as well. But that's completely up to you," she said, pointing at Sarah.

"You mean up to *us*," Sarah said.

"No, sweetie, I mean *you*. In this world," she said, gesturing through the last set of doors, "the women are in control."

Sarah looked over at Jack, stuck her tongue out, and smiled.

"One last thing," Tiffany said. "No means no, and nothing short of clear and obvious consent means yes. Break those rules and you'll be introduced to a lifetime ban and possibly a rough walk out to the curb."

Sarah grabbed Jack's arm. "Do you mind if we skip the rest of the tour? Let's go get a drink and dance?"

Jack looked at Tiffany, seemingly seeking her approval.

"It's whatever you want," Tiffany said. "If you decide later you want to head to the back rooms, I can either guide you, or you can jump in without me. Either way, let the bartenders know so they can transfer your alcohol to the back."

"Thanks," Sarah said, gently nudging Jack to walk back the way they came. "Because your girlfriend wants to dance."

CHAPTER SEVEN

Jack slumped down into a chair. "Uncle. I give. I'm tapping out," he said with a smile. "I haven't danced this much since our wedding night."

Sarah walked up beside him and looked at herself in the floor-to-ceiling mirror on the wall. She was a little drunk. They both were. "Hey, boyfriend," she said, still looking at herself.

Jack laughed. "Yes, Mrs. 26544," he said, citing their membership number.

"I can't remember the last time I had this much fun," she said.

"That makes two of us," Jack said as he pulled her down onto his lap.

Sarah wrapped her arms around his neck and kissed him. Then softly, she said, "And I hate to admit it, but I look fucking hot in this dress."

"Yes, you do," he said.

"And Jack?" she whispered between kisses.

"Yeah?"

"I assume if this is a sex club, there is a room behind

those big doors by the condom bowl where you can make love with me?"

"There are several rooms back there that meet that description. In fact, I already have one picked out for the evening. It's the whole reason we're here."

She pulled her head away from him, far enough to focus on his face. "And what room is that?" she asked.

"A big room where lots of people can watch."

She cocked her head sideways.

"Fantasy number one: have sex in public," he said as he pulled her head to him and kissed her.

"Is that how this is going play out?" she said, kissing him back.

"Yes."

"Are you sure you know what you are doing?" she said, kissing him again.

"I'm sure."

Sarah kissed him one more time and stood up. "Geronimo," she said, taking his hand.

Jack smiled and stood up. "Do you want me to grab Tiffany?"

Sarah made eye contact with one of the bartenders and pointed to the back room. He smiled and nodded. Sarah started walking in the direction of the locker rooms. "I think we can figure it out ourselves," she said.

Jack's jaw dropped when Sarah paused just inside the locker room and stepped out of her dress. Standing naked, she handed it to the attendant and gave her their membership number. Wrapping a towel around herself, Sarah looked back at Jack. "I don't care what the policy is; I'm not going back there without my shoes on." Staring at Jack, she added, "Are you coming?"

Jack walked over to their locker and began to undress. Sarah threw him a towel once he was naked, and they headed for the back room. They paused just a moment before Sarah pushed the door open so they could step through. The initial room was a bar area much like the front room, but half the clientele was naked, and the other half was in either skimpy lingerie or wrapped in towels. Off in the corners, a few people engaged in one form of sex or another.

"Drink," Jack said quickly.

"Please," Sarah replied.

Once they had a beverage in hand, they ventured further into the back, wandering down a couple of halls with doors on both sides. Jack and Sarah could hear people having sex on the other side of the doors. The look on Sarah and Jack's faces was such that an attractive thirty-something African American woman said, "They're private rooms."

"So, anyone can use them?" Sarah asked.

"Sure. One of you. Two of you. Six of you," the woman said, smiling. "The important thing is that you get to decide who and how many...and it's more discrete than the public playrooms."

"Public playrooms?" Sarah asked.

The woman laughed. "What in the world have you two gotten yourselves into?" She grabbed Sarah's hand. "My name is Linda. Come with me." Walking to the end of the hallway, Linda paused and pointed to the left. "*Public playrooms.*"

Sarah leaned forward just enough to look into the room. There were four or five couples, all at various stages of having sex. She had never been in a room with other people having sex before. She couldn't take her eyes off them. The sights. The sounds. It was incredible. Linda pulled Jack up so he could see as well. After watching the two of them staring for a minute, Linda put her arm over Sarah's shoulder and pointed to a space in the middle of the room. "Go," she said. "Why are you waiting? Go." With a smile, she gave them each a nudge.

Sarah looked up at Jack and smiled. He took her by the hand and led her out to the middle of the room. Spreading out both of their towels, he gestured for her to lie down. For a moment, all Sarah could think about was the image of her husband standing in the middle of a room full of people with an erection, and not a soul seemed to find it strange. She laid down on the center of the towels and pulled him down with her.

Kissing him, she whispered, "Are we really doing this?"

"Yes," he said.

"Jack, it feels so weird."

He slowly ran his hand up her leg, where his fingers found wetness he hadn't felt in a long time. "Something tells me you like it," he said.

"I love it," she confessed.

"Because it feels wrong?" he asked, knowing the answer.

"It does, doesn't it? I can't stop watching everyone."

"Then watch. It's why everyone's here."

Sarah rolled Jack onto his back and began kissing her way down his chest. As she made her way past his stomach, she noticed a couple lying in front of them in a mirror image position. Her partner and Jack were lying almost head-to-head, like two hands on some giant clock that read six pm. Sarah paused just above Jack's cock, and for a moment, she froze as she watched the other woman take her partner into her mouth. Before Sarah knew it, the woman looked up and saw Sarah watching. Sarah looked away, embarrassed, but the other woman just smiled and eagerly returned her attention to her partner. With that, whatever apprehension Sarah had before was gone. If others were going to watch her, she decided she better put on a show.

About a minute into Sarah's performance, Jack pulled her head away. "Sarah, you are killing me," he said.

Sarah quickly climbed up and mounted him.

"Slow," Jack cautioned.

When the woman in front of them saw Sarah riding Jack, she too climbed up on her partner. Sarah couldn't take her eyes off them. She locked eyes with the stranger, and their thrusting quickly fell into sync. They shared a grin as the pace quickened. Sarah could tell that Jack wasn't going to last much longer, so she changed the angle she was moving to one of her favorites and drove her pelvis in to meet his thrust. After a moment, she leaned down on his chest, closed her eyes, and let out a long, guttural moan as she and Jack orgasmed together.

Jack couldn't tell what or who had Sarah so enamored, but he didn't care. Watching her get off watching someone else was the most erotic thing he had ever seen. Sarah collapsed onto his chest.

"My God," she said, catching her breath. "I was wrong."

"What's the matter?" he asked, confused and struggling for air himself.

"You were right," she said, panting.

"About what?"

"Fuck adequate," she said.

Jack laughed and hugged her close. "Geronimo," he yelled out to a room full of naked strangers.

CHAPTER EIGHT

Jack was lying in the hotel bed with images from the evening running through his head. Sarah walked out of the bathroom wearing nothing but her new strand of pearls, turned off the lights, and walked over to the window. Jack's eyes had just begun to adjust to the darkness when Sarah opened the curtains, and the city lights lit up the room through the wall-to-wall, floor-to-ceiling windows. From the sixty-eighth floor, it felt like they could see the entire city—and the entire city could see them.

Sarah bent over the railing that ran the length of the window and wiggled her ass at Jack. "Hey, want to make love with your girlfriend while the entire city of New York watches?" She didn't have to ask a second time.

Sarah had come twice at the club. Making love with Jack looking out over the city would be her third in one day. Life can change on a dime, she thought to herself. She tried to imagine what other surprises her future held. But there would be plenty of time to obsess over that later. Tonight? Tonight, she just wanted to fuck her boyfriend.

CHAPTER NINE

Sarah had a fleeting moment of guilt the first time she saw her son after their night in Manhattan. She couldn't put her finger on it, but the feeling passed as she slipped effortlessly back into Mommy Mode. Lucky for Jack, she didn't get stuck there. The night in New York elevated their sex life to new heights over the weeks that followed. They didn't go back to Lux, but they certainly brought Lux memories back with them. To their bedroom. And laundry room. And even once to the car parked in the garage.

A month to the day after their night out on the town, Jack handed Sarah a small, neatly wrapped present while seated in a romantic French restaurant in the Upper East Side. "For you," he said.

"Should I be nervous?" Sarah asked.

"Probably. It was a recommendation from Brooke."

"Size Two, Brooke? From the sex shop?" Sarah asked, holding the package away from her as if it might explode.

"The one and only," Jack said, unable to suppress the grin on his face.

"Geronimo Brooke?"

"Absolutely. She hasn't steered us wrong yet."

Sarah slowly pulled the ribbon off the present while giving Jack a dirty look. "I didn't realize the two of you had become pals."

"Well, not sure I would say pals, but I needed some assistance for this evening and wasn't sure who else to turn to."

"Ok, now I really am nervous."

"Geronimo, baby."

Sarah cautiously unwrapped the present and slowly peeked into the box. "Is this what I think it is?"

"If you think that it's a vibrator that snaps into place and is turned on and off by remote control, then yes. It's exactly what you think it is," Jack said, tipping back his wine glass.

"'Snaps' into place? Really?"

"Brooke's word, not mine."

Sarah closed the box and pushed it to the middle of the table. Lifting her glass of wine to her lips and taking a sip, she looked across the table at Jack but said nothing.

"What?" Jack asked with a smile.

"You think you're cute, don't you?" Sarah asked with a smile she couldn't suppress.

Jack leaned in and smiled. "If you think this is cute, just wait."

"Wait for what, Jack?" Sarah asked.

"Wait until you get back from snapping that in place," he said, pointing to the back corner of the restaurant. "The ladies' room is that way."

Sarah placed her wine glass down and looked into the box again. "Jack, seriously? This isn't me."

"You're telling me the woman who masturbates in the carpool lane is above this?" Jack said, leaning back in his chair and looking across the restaurant at the bar.

"That's not fair."

"Does it seem a little vulgar?"

"Yes."

"Over the top sexual?"

"Yes."

Jack leaned in and looked her directly in the eyes. "Does it feel wrong?"

Sarah let out an almost imperceivable laugh. "Yeah, it does."

Jack smiled and picked up his glass of wine. "The ladies' room is that way," he said, looking towards the bar.

"You win," she said, standing up from the table. Walking by Jack on the way to the bathroom, she leaned in and kissed him. "You are cute, though."

"I know."

A few minutes later, Sarah emerged from the bathroom, making funny faces as she walked. Gingerly taking her seat, Sarah looked up and smiled. Leaning in, she whispered, "I'm not going to lie. It's a damn turn on wearing this in front of all these people."

"You don't need to whisper," Jack said. "While you were in the bathroom, I told everyone about the vibrator."

"Not funny," she said, giving him a dirty look that quickly transformed into an intense one. She grabbed the edge of the table as if she were having labor pains. "Jesus, that's way too much."

"What's too much?"

"The vibrator is way too strong. Can you turn it down?"

Jack laughed. "That may be harder than you think."

Sarah was almost doubled over. Without realizing it, she closed her eyes and fought to suppress the small noises that emerged from her. It wasn't clear to anyone within range to hear if the noises were pain or pleasure, but it was clear to all that the noises didn't belong in a restaurant.

"I'm trying," Jack reassured her.

Sarah opened her eyes and spoke through clenched teeth. "Jack, either turn it down or fucking turn it off."

Jack took his hand and passed it across his throat, giving the universal cut it sign. Instantly the vibration stopped. And instantly, realization spread across Sarah's face.

"Are you kidding me right now?" she asked as she glared at Jack. "Who has the fucking remote?"

Jack bowed his head. "Let's just say...a stranger."

Sarah filled her wine glass and took a big sip. After a moment, she finally spoke. "Jack, you literally just let a stranger stimulate me without my consent."

"Jesus, Sarah, it's not like that," Jack blurted out.

"Then tell me how you see it."

"You know very well that the next fantasy on your list is being tied to a bed and having a stranger go down on you. This is tame compared to that."

Sarah leaned back in her chair and tried casually to scan the restaurant for Jack's coconspirator. "Jack, this was never my idea. This is all you."

"We talked about this. You agreed to it," Jack pleaded.

"I didn't agree to this. And even if I had agreed to it, I reserve the right to change my mind."

Jack leaned forward and took her hands. "I am so sorry. I would never in a million years do something on purpose to hurt you. I understand this isn't exactly what we talked about, but I honestly thought it would turn you on."

"The vibrator, yes. It being operated by someone I've never met? With no warning? No." She let go of his hands and leaned back in her chair. "How was the rest of the night supposed to play out?" she asked.

"Excuse me?"

"Is this person the stranger you intended to have go down on me? Later tonight, I presume?"

"That was the plan."

"And where exactly did you find this person, if you don't mind me asking?"

"Brooke."

"Of course, Brooke," Sarah said, shaking her head.

"Babe, Brooke obviously has a lot of experience with this. When I brought it up, she didn't hesitate. She said this was our guy. When I reached out and spoke with him, he sounded perfect. I met him for drinks one day last week, and we really hit it off."

Sarah sat shaking her head. "Well, plans change, Jack," she said taking a sip of wine. "Let's get him over here."

"Excuse me?"

"If you would like to salvage anything of this evening, you better pull up another chair and get him over here."

Jack sat frozen in place.

"Let's get moving. I'm starving and, surprisingly, getting fairly horny so...lets go."

"So, you forgive me?"

"You hurt my feelings. So, forgiven? Yes. Forgotten? Not even close."

"I'll take what I can get," Jack said as he left to find the maître d' to request that they accommodate another guest at their table. After a quick exchange, Jack walked over and spoke briefly with a handsome man seated at the far side of the bar. The men looked like two guilty school kids as they walked over to Sarah.

Sarah stood to greet them. "I hope you know what you're doing," she said as they approached.

"Sarah, this is Marcus. Marcus, this is my wife, Sarah," Jack said as calmly as possible.

"Hi, Sarah, it's nice to meet you," Marcus said, offering his hand.

Sarah leaned in past his hand and kissed him on the

cheek. "You stimulated my vagina, Marcus. The least you can do is kiss me."

Marcus choked trying to get words out of his mouth. "This is true."

A couple of employees appeared with an additional place setting. When they began to set them next to Jack, Sarah quickly interrupted. "Let's place those next to me, please," she said, quickly turning to Jack with a slightly cocked head. "I mean, if that's okay with you?"

"Absolutely," Jack said.

Marcus waited for Sarah to sit before taking his place to her left.

"Wine?" Jack asked, holding the bottle of Bordeaux just above Marcus's glass.

"Please," he said.

Sarah turned to face Marcus. "If you don't mind, may I please have the remote?"

Marcus raced to get the remote out of his jacket pocket. "Yes, I'm sorry. Here, take it..." he said, gently handing the device over to Sarah.

Sarah took a moment to inspect it. She pressed a button and immediately received the same intense stimulation as before. It took only a second for her to find the controls to reduce the intensity. After a moment, a small smile spread across her face as she closed her eyes. She reached down and grabbed Marcus's thigh. "Much better," she said as she finally turned it off. "Here," she said. "You can have this back now," she said, offering it to Marcus.

Marcus's face looked like he was afraid it was a trap, but Sarah handed it over without incident.

"Now," Sarah said, looking at the menu, "the sooner we get through this meal, the sooner you boys can get on with the main course."

Jack and Marcus exchanged a quick look, a quick smile, and both grabbed a menu.

Throughout the meal, Sarah peppered Marcus with questions about his life. He grew up in New Hampshire but moved to New York to attend Columbia University, where he received a degree in Finance. Marcus admitted that the most challenging thing about Columbia was getting in, which was a good thing because he invested most of his time in Rugby and the newfound pleasures of big city living. He confessed that he had an extremely high libido which presented challenges over the years. In his experience, the initial honeymoon phase of a new relationship typically waned after three or four months. When the disparity of sexual needs created more conflict in the relationship than the joy he got from it, he thought it best for both parties to move on. He didn't want to be unfaithful, but he wasn't willing to put something that important on the back burner. He knew it sounded selfish, but he thought it was better for everyone if he left before resentment grew rather than love. It was a next-door neighbor who enlightened him on being a bull for other couples.

"A bull? As in for breeding?" Sarah asked.

"Well, that is the implication, but it simply means a single male in the swinging lifestyle," Marcus said.

"And dare I ask what they would call a single woman in the swinging lifestyle?" Sarah asked.

"A unicorn," Marcus replied.

"Because they don't exist?" Sarah asked with a laugh.

Marcus smiled. "Oh no, they exist. But they are magical creatures who are difficult to find."

"And your next-door neighbor, is he a bull?"

"Actually, Brooke is my next-door neighbor," he said.

"Ah, and the circle is complete," Sarah said.

She took her last bite of the meal and placed her silverware across her plate. "I am ready when you are," she said to nobody in particular, neatly folding her napkin and placing it on the table.

The cab ride to the hotel was long enough for Sarah's nerves to begin to get to her. Drilling Marcus with questions had distracted her from the reality of the moment. With her thighs pressing against a man on each side of her, the long cab ride to the village gave her plenty of time to dwell on what they were about to do. Walking into the main hotel lobby, Sarah turned and hugged Marcus. Pointing to the bar, she said, "If you wouldn't mind, please wait for Jack and me to have a quick chat?"

Marcus smiled. "No worries, and...no pressure. I'm happy to go have a drink." After taking a few steps toward the bar, he stopped and turned around. "Hey, just in case I don't see you again tonight," he said, tossing the vibrator remote to Jack, "It was fun."

Jack laughed. "Ditto."

"And Sarah, it was a pleasure to meet you," he said. With that, he turned and continued to the bar.

Jack gave Sarah a funny look. "I honestly forgot that he had that."

"I didn't," Sarah said as she took Jack's hand and headed for the elevators.

"Wait, you mean...." Jack said, waiting for her to complete his thought.

"Oh yeah," Sarah said.

"Really? Are we talking a little? A lot?"

"Let's just say I'm very impressed with the batteries and that I would like for you to walk faster."

Riding up in the elevator, Sarah turned and hugged Jack. "Are you sure you know what you're doing? Are you sure you want to open this door? Pandora's Box? Genie's bottle? After this, I don't think we will ever be able to get back to this place in our marriage."

Jack pulled back from their hug and kissed her. "I love you with all my heart. And as far as I am concerned, we jumped off that ledge about a month ago, and now we should just enjoy the fall."

The elevator beeped, and the door opened. Sarah led the way toward their suite. "It's not the fall I'm worried about, Jack. What concerns me is the landing."

CHAPTER TEN

Jack greeted Marcus with a nervous smile when he opened the door to their suite. He attempted to shake his hand before realizing that Marcus had a wine bucket with champagne in one hand and three champagne flutes precariously held in the other. Jack quickly took two glasses and stood aside to let Marcus in. Walking to the middle of the room, Marcus could see into the bedroom at the end of the suite. Sarah was on her back in the middle of a king-sized bed, blindfolded, with her arms bound to each side of the headboard. She was wearing a thin top that buttoned up the front. The material was sheer enough to reveal the absence of a bra and the presence of beautiful breasts.

Marcus turned to Jack and nodded to the bedroom. Jack smiled, nodded, and led the way. Once they were in the bedroom, Marcus placed the ice bucket on a table by the bed. He looked down at Sarah and smiled, slowly removing the foil from the bottle. A moment later, he sent the champagne cork flying across the room with a pop.

"Jack?" Sarah said in a nervous voice.

"Right here, babe," Jack said, reassuring her.

Marcus carefully filled three glasses of champagne, handed one to Jack, and took another to the side of the bed. Carefully cradling the back of Sarah's neck, Marcus lifted her head to bring her lips to meet the champagne glass.

"Careful," he said as she took a sip. A small amount of champagne ran out of the corner of her mouth and down her cheek. She couldn't help but smile. Marcus laid her head down and gently traced his thumb up her cheek, wiping off the champagne. He placed her glass down on the nightstand. Retrieving his glass, he held it in the air in Jack's direction. Jack raised his glass to meet him in the middle for a toast.

Sarah was restless on the bed. Gently pulling against the restraints with her arms, she also seemed to pull against restraints that weren't on her legs, rubbing her feet up and down against the bed covers. Marcus put his glass down and walked to the right side of the bed, leaving Jack with a clear view. Sitting on the bed next to Sarah, he ran his fingers through her hair, tucking a soft brunette strand behind her ear. Once it was exposed, Marcus gently rubbed her earlobe. Sarah's reaction was to tilt her head into a raised shoulder, as Jack knew that ears were a Sarah hotspot.

Without taking his attention off of his efforts with Sarah, Marcus looked at Jack, made a quizzical face, pointed to the ceiling, and mouthed the word music. Jack nodded and disappeared into the other room.

"Sarah, how are you doing?" Marcus asked in little more than a whisper.

"I'm okay," she said.

"Okay? I think Jack was hoping for a bit more than okay," he said, standing up from the bed and taking a sip of champagne.

"I mean, I'm nervous, but...I feel okay with everything so far."

"Do you feel safe?" Marcus asked.

Sarah was quiet for a second before responding. "I do," she said, ironically pulling on the restraints as she answered.

Light jazz started playing softly from the suite's living area as Marcus once again supported Sarah to help her take another sip of champagne. Placing the glass down, he sat by her side. He reached across her and slowly stroked the outside of her leg from her ankle to her hip and back down. After a moment, he repeated the movement, but this time on the inside of her leg. As his fingers approached the top of her inner thigh, Sarah took a quick, sharp breath. Marcus ran his thumb just inside her underwear and followed the cloth over her hip.

"Jack?" Sarah asked in an anxious voice.

"I'm right here," Jack said, sitting in a chair off to the side. "You okay?"

Sarah hesitated before answering. "I would be better if you were here, maybe holding my hand." She turned her head to look in Marcus's direction. "Is that okay with you?"

Marcus let out a gentle laugh. "Sarah, this is all for you, and it can be whatever you want it to be."

"Thank you," Sarah said, followed quickly by, "Jack. Hand. Now."

Jack smiled at Marcus and quickly complied, sitting on the bed and taking Sarah's hand in his own. Sarah gave him a firm squeeze before relaxing her grip a bit. Jack met her with equal pressure as he began to run his fingers through her hair with the other hand.

Marcus traced his hand from Sarah's ear, gently down the side of her neck and through what cleavage was visible. Sarah's grip tightened on Jack's hand as Marcus's hand approached her breasts. Lifting his hand, he glanced up at Jack and paused long enough to make sure he was doing okay. Jack just returned a smile and looked down at his wife with what appeared to be a bizarre look of love, lust, and pride. Sarah was a beautiful woman, but seeing her tied up, half-naked, responding to another man's touch was more erotic than he'd ever imagined.

Marcus laid down on his side next to Sarah and slowly unbuttoned her top. After each button, he would reach down and lightly stroke the newly revealed skin with the back of his fingers. Sarah continued to pull on the restraints and bite her lower lip.

Once her shirt was completely unbuttoned, Marcus pulled the fabric away, leaving her breasts exposed. Jack could see her breath quicken. She squeezed Jack's hand as the moment came and went for the expected stimulation. Instead, Marcus reached down and firmly pressed his hand against Sarah's vagina. Her reaction was an instinctive effort to cover herself, but the action simply lifted her knees up and her head off the bed.

Jack could see the desire building in Sarah. He realized that even though he had made love with Sarah a thousand times, he was strangely too close to it to witness this erotic, physical dance that she was engaged in. It was surreal for Jack to see his wife's chest expand with each breath and her hands tightly gripping the rope that held her in place; to watch as her breath quickened and her pelvis thrust to meet the stimulation she so craved from another man.

Marcus held his hand completely still. Sarah's movements and sounds took on a tone that was a combination of pleading and impatience. Sarah began to thrust harder against his hand. Marcus gave a wry smile to Jack as if this was the moment he had been waiting for all along. For a few seconds,

Marcus withdrew his hand every time she thrust. And he followed her when she withdrew. Marcus met Sarah with equal pressure, pulling away from her thrust and pressing in when she pulled back. Finally, he removed his hand altogether.

"Oh, dear lord," Sarah said under her breath.

Marcus leaned over her, positioning his mouth just a fraction of an inch above hers. It only took a moment for her to feel his presence, and she raised her head until their lips met. Kissing passionately, Marcus firmly grabbed her breast and gently squeezed her nipple between his thumb and index finger.

Part of Jack felt like he was watching a movie, but Sarah's firm grasp of his hand kept him present in the moment. Adrenaline was rushing through him in a manner he would never be able to explain. Watching Sarah passionately kiss Marcus, looking at her nipples, his wife's nipples, respond to another man's touch was surreal and exciting and breathtaking and terrifying. If he had any doubts in that moment, they weren't conscious in his thoughts. And his ever-present erection made its thoughts pretty clear on the situation.

Marcus slowly kissed his way down Sarah's neck to her breasts. Rubbing one nipple with his fingers, he gradually found his way to the other nipple with his mouth.

Sarah seemed to be fighting her moans. They were restrained just below the surface.

"Jack?" Sarah asked. "Are you okay? Are we good?"

Jack leaned over her and kissed her. "We are amazing," he said. He kissed her again and whispered in her ear, "The only way I could be any better is if you would stop holding back and allow yourself to enjoy this."

She squeezed his hand. "Are you sure? It's really okay?"

"It's better than okay, baby. It's fucking amazing."

With that, Jack sat back down and continued to hold her hand.

Marcus kissed and licked his way down to Sarah's belly button. Still lying by her side, he reached under her closest leg and brought his hand to her vagina. Slipping his thumb inside her underwear, Marcus rubbed gentle circles on and around her clit.

Sarah let out a loud moan as she thrust her pelvis up into his hand.

"That a girl," Jack said, squeezing her hand.

When Marcus thought she was approaching orgasm, he quickly stopped.

"Motherfucker," Sarah yelled out, half laughing.

Marcus laughed. "Don't worry, Sarah. It's coming." He leaned down and gently pulled her panties from her body. Taking a position at the foot of the bed, he firmly grabbed each leg. Spreading them just enough so he fit between them, kneeling, he held one leg high off the bed and began to kiss the inside of her ankle.

As Jack watched another man spread his wife's legs and hover over her exposed vagina, his thoughts were such that he should bring this all to a stop, but every fiber in his body couldn't wait to see this through.

Marcus slowly kissed his way down her leg until he rested himself on his elbows and gently breathed out warm air on her thigh, just an inch from her vagina.

The noises coming out of Sarah were pushing Jack closer and closer to exploding without any physical stimulation.

Marcus slowly moved the gentle warm breath up Sarah's thigh and over her throbbing clit. Every time he breathed out, Sarah would lift her pelvis, trying to make contact. After a few minutes of cat-and-mouse teasing, Marcus wrapped his left hand around her leg and pressed down just above her vagina. With his right hand, he reached up and firmly grabbed her breast. The next time Sarah thrust her pelvis to him, he drew her clit into his mouth. Rather than running from her, Marcus kept his mouth perfectly still, licking and sucking whatever Sarah brought to him. Moving, thrusting, gyrating, it was all up to her.

It only took a moment before she began to plead with Jack.

"Jack, I want to come."

Jack leaned in and ran his fingers through the hair over her ear. "Baby, I told you, I want you to come."

"Fuck, are you sure? Really, really sure?"

"One hundred percent. Come for me. Come for Marcus."

"Kiss me."

Jack leaned over her, cradled her head in his hand, and kissed her.

Sarah pulled firmly against the restraints as a moan escaped through their kissing. Jack held her through an intense series of muscle contractions.

Marcus gently kissed Sarah's clit one more time. He looked up and smiled as he watched Jack cradling his wife's head. "Well, that was fun," he said, smiling at them.

Marcus rolled off the end of the bed and stood up. He walked over to the nightstand and finished his glass of champagne. "You're a lucky man, Jack." Marcus leaned over the bed and kissed Sarah, who was still trying to catch her breath. She could taste herself on his lips. She just had the most erotic orgasm ever, which made her crave more.

"You, my dear, are an amazing woman," Marcus said, leaning in for one more kiss. "Thank you for trusting me...and Jack."

"You boys better not leave me like this," she said.

"Sorry, babe, you ready to be untied?" Jack asked.

"Hell no," she said. "I'm ready for someone to fuck me."

Jack had been teetering on orgasm through this whole

affair. Listening to his wife, bound to a bed, blindfolded, speaking like that almost put him over the edge. He looked up at Marcus to see his reaction.

Marcus just smiled and gently grabbed one of Sarah's ankles. "As nice as that sounds, I think this is probably a good point in the evening for you two to spend a little time alone."

"Are you sure?" Jack asked. "It appears you're welcome to stay."

Marcus walked over and shook Jack's hand. "No, but thank you." Reaching down and rubbing her leg again, he said, "You, young lady, are adorable. If you two ever want to have a Round Two, you know how to find me."

Jack started to stand up, but Marcus held his hand up to stop him. Pointing at Sarah, he just smiled. "You kids have fun," he said as he turned and walked to let himself out.

Jack quickly removed his clothes and climbed up between Sarah's legs, but in that moment, he froze. He looked down at his wife and did his best to burn the image into his memory banks.

"Jack, what are you doing?" she asked.

"Just looking at how ridiculously hot my girlfriend looks right now."

Sarah let out a groan. "Please…"

"Did you really want to sleep with him tonight?"

"Does it look like I want to talk right now? Please don't ruin the moment. Get over here and fuck me."

Lifting her legs, Jack gently entered her. He was not surprised at how wet she was. He tried his best to go slow, but there was no point.

"I'm sorry," Jack said, thrusting with each word. "I can't help it," he said as he held her in his arms.

"It's okay. Come."

A moment later, Jack came and collapsed onto her. It took a couple of minutes to catch his breath and eventually untie her. Curled up together in bed, drinking the rest of the champagne, they discussed the night's events. As the evening drew to a close, Sarah got up, turned out the lights, and opened the curtains once again to invite the whole world to watch her make love with her boyfriend

CHAPTER ELEVEN

"Hi, Jack."

"Hello, Monica," Jack said, walking through the kitchen without making eye contact. He saw her car parked out front when he got home from work, so he was prepared for her presence. Monica wasn't all that bad, but something about her was emotionally draining for Jack. She was tiring.

"I was just asking your lovely wife what you two were up to."

"Oh yeah," Jack said, leaning in to kiss Sarah. "Not sure what you're talking about," he said as he walked over to grab a beer out of the fridge.

Monica walked over to the bar and refilled her glass of vodka. "You two think you're so cute. But you don't realize that by saying nothing at all, it simply leaves it up to my imagination."

"Well, again, I'm not sure what point you're trying to make, but I would be careful not to let that imagination of yours run wild." He walked up behind Sarah and rubbed her shoulders. "Unless, of course, Sarah here has something she isn't sharing with me. In which case, I would like to know as well. Sarah? You have something you want to share with us?"

"I think I've overshared already. Thanks."

Monica sat on a barstool across from Sarah at the island in the middle of their kitchen. "See, that right there. What exactly did you share with Jack?"

"Good lord, Monica, mind your business," Sarah said with a laugh as she stood up and hugged Jack. "Colin is in the den. He can't wait to show you the new rocket ship he built out of Legos."

Sarah walked to the fridge and pulled some food out to prepare dinner as Jack went to find Colin.

Monica fidgeted for a second in her seat, staring into her glass of vodka. "If I guess will you tell me?"

"No," Sarah said as she began to slice chicken on a cutting board.

"So, there is something to tell?" Monica pressed.

"I didn't say that."

"Sure you did."

Sarah stopped cutting the chicken and held the knife up with the point in Monica's direction. "Monica, there is nothing to tell," she said through a faint smile.

Monica got up from the stool and lay down across a love seat next to a big bay window overlooking the backyard. "I feel like we're at a great party, and you have a big bag of cocaine, but you won't share it with me."

"I've never done cocaine, so maybe that isn't a great analogy."

"Well, you don't have to do cocaine to know that not sharing isn't nice, especially when it comes to something that has put a smile on your face for the past two months. I've never seen you and Jack this happy or loving in all the years I've known you."

"Well, maybe we've just hit our stride."

"Sure, and maybe I'm the Easter Bunny."

Sarah continued to prepare dinner as she tried to change the subject. "How are things in your life?"

Monica got off the love seat and walked behind Sarah. She grabbed a handful of carrots that Sarah had just peeled and sat back down on the barstool. Between crunches, she quickly summed up her current state of relationships.

"Bob's still dead. Fred's still an asshole. And the only men I find interesting enough to sleep with aren't bright enough to carry on an adult conversation after the fact."

"It can't be that bad."

"Oh dear, it is. Be happy you're in here with your perfect little husband and not out there in the digital dating world. I thought pickup bars were bad, yet somehow, this swipe-left-swipe-right world is even worse."

Sarah wanted to believe that Monica was exaggerating, but a brief thought of dating today sent a shiver up her spine. Monica married relatively young to the man of her dreams, Bob. Sadly, he got colon cancer and passed away at thirty-two, many years before anyone thought to worry about such things. A few years later, she married a much older man who had plenty of money and even more insecurities. She lived under his thumb for years dealing with so many accusations of affairs that it ultimately drove her to have a real one, bringing the marriage to Fred to an ugly, foregone conclusion.

"You should move to Alaska," Jack said, having come into the room on the tail-end of the conversation. "I hear the odds would be forever in your favor," he said.

"Cute, Jack," Monica said. "By the way, Sarah let me in on your little secret."

"No, she didn't," he replied in a sing-song voice.

"Yes, she did," Monica parroted back in the same singing manner.

"No, Monica, she didn't," Jack said in a matter-of-fact tone.

"How can you be so sure?" Monica asked.

Jack walked around and grabbed another beer out of the fridge. "I know she didn't because first there is nothing to tell."

"And second?" Monica asked.

"And second," Jack said as he paused in the door on his way back to play with Colin, "had she told you, when I got back in here, you wouldn't be discussing the trials and tribulations of your sex life." With that, he disappeared down the hall with a grin.

"I hate you both," Monica yelled after him. She looked back at Sarah, who was busy chopping vegetables trying to suppress a smile. "What exactly could you two be hiding that seems to make you so happy, yet you aren't willing to share it with your best friend?"

"Let's get back to the Alaska discussion, please. I think there's some promise there," Sarah said quickly, trying to change the subject once again.

"You won the lottery?"

"I wish," Sarah replied.

"Jack got promoted to senior director."

"Yes, two years ago."

Monica sat there pulling on her earlobe, trying to think what else it could be.

"Alaska, please?" Sarah asked.

"You got drunk in the city and had a threesome?"

Sarah didn't mean to stop chopping vegetables. But she did, only for a second. The question seemed to paralyze her. Without looking up, she said, "Absolutely not." But it was too late. The damage was done. That was all it took for Monica to see the truth.

Hopping from the barstool, Monica ran over and put her arm over Sarah's shoulder. "You little minx, you. Are you kidding me?"

Sarah glanced over her shoulder towards the den. "Monica, stop it," she said.

"Guy-guy-girl or girl-girl-guy?" Monica implored.

"What are you talking about?" Sarah asked.

"Who did you add to the party? A guy or a girl?"

Sarah put the knife down and looked Monica in the eye. "I am begging you to leave this alone. Please?"

Monica filled Sarah's glass of wine and held her glass of vodka in the air to toast. "To my best friend, Sarah, the perfect preppy, proper, yet perverted Connecticut housewife. Cheers!"

Sarah toasted with her, but the death stare she gave Monica made it clear that was the end of the discussion.

"I'm not sure why you're making it such a big deal," Monica said. "Bob and I had a lot of them. Generally, when we were on vacation, though. I guess it was mainly an island thing for us."

Sarah tried not to take the bait, but she couldn't help it. "Guy-guy-girl or girl-girl-guy?"

Monica got a huge smile and leaned close. "You go first," she whispered.

"Guy," Sarah said through a blushing smile. "A big, beautiful, rugged, gentle, talented guy."

"Oh my. Good for you," Monica said. "And way to go, Jack."

"And you?" Sarah asked.

"We tried both, but without question, I preferred adding a man to the mix."

"Really?"

"Absolutely. Women can outlast a man every time. Why in

the world would I want someone around to help me wear him out faster?"

"Well, unless you wanted to spend time with a woman," Sarah said.

Monica put her drink on the counter and made a shocked face. "Well, Sarah Williams, is there something you want to tell me?"

Sarah turned red and quickly carried the food she prepped over to the stove.

"That's not what I meant."

"That's exactly what you meant," Monica insisted.

"Sarah is pretty good at speaking her mind," Jack said, startling the women as he snuck into the kitchen to grab another beer. "If she said that's not what she meant, I'm betting that's not what she meant."

"Thanks for the support, Jack," Sarah said, not turning around from the stove to face him.

Jack turned to Monica. "By the way, what didn't she mean?"

"Jack, at this point, I'm so confused I don't even remember what we were talking about."

"Well, sorry for the interruption. Please continue," Jack said, walking back down the hall.

After about ten seconds of silence, Sarah turned around wide-eyed at Monica. She pointed her finger down the hall towards Jack. "That would not be good," she whispered.

"Fine," Monica said. "But next time we go out for lunch, I will need details."

"We'll see," Sarah said. She realized that it was a risk for Monica to know anything about the list and their recent activities. But the truth was that Sarah had been dying to talk with someone about it all along. She wanted to share all of the details and emotions. It was the most exciting thing that had happened to her in years, possibly ever, and she couldn't tell a soul. What Sarah really wanted to do was climb up on the rooftops and scream it to the world. Ironically, none of this would have ever happened had it not been for Monica and her damn tequila. Maybe it was only fitting that Sarah let her into the circle of trust.

CHAPTER TWELVE

"I'll say this, Jack. If nothing else, you have a lot of balls," Greg Taylor said, leaning against the squash court wall, trying to catch his breath.

"I don't know why you say that. That was a close one," Jack replied.

Greg leaned back against the wall and slowly slid down until he was seated on the court floor. "You're too smart to humiliate your boss, but you're too competitive to throw the game."

"That's not true. You win a lot of games," Jack said as he hit the ball to himself off of the front wall.

"Jack, I beat you two games every match. And we always play best of five. To make matters worse, you win the last game by two points. Every time." Greg wiped the sweat off his forehead with the sweatband on his wrist. "You toy with me, Jack. In a way, it's a slow form of humiliation, possibly worse than an outright beating."

"Come on, Greg."

"I think it must take a great deal of both control and concentration to beat me like that so consistently."

After gently lobbing the ball off the front wall, Jack caught it with his hand. "Mr. Taylor, I was ranked top ten in New England three out of four years of prep school, number one my senior year. I'm also twenty-plus years younger than you. And..." he hesitated.

"And what?" Greg asked, annoyed.

"And, I don't like to lose," he said.

Greg began to hit the side of his foot with the edge of his racket. "I'm aware. The last bit there is why you work for one of the top private equity firms in the world. I don't hire losers."

Jack began to hit the ball off the front wall again.

"Speaking of which, Jack, your trading has been a bit out of character over the last few months."

Jack immediately turned to his boss, letting the ball fly by. "What do you mean out of character? I've made more money for the company over the last two months than any other time."

"This is true, and I have the reports to prove it."

Jack walked in front of Greg and looked down. "It's not out of character for me to make you money. So, what gives?"

"You've just been a tad aggressive lately. When I brought you into the firm, you were the wunderkind of value investing. Long-term value. Lately, it seems you are drifting out of your lane."

"Is this a Nick Leeson speech?" Jack asked, citing the trader who collapsed the oldest merchant bank in the United Kingdom by making riskier and riskier trades trying to get out of the financial hole he had dug.

"God no," Greg said as he struggled to stand. Jack reached out, grabbed his hand, and helped Greg to his feet. "It's just my job to stay on top of things. I'm just curious if there was something in your life or something you saw in the market that is affecting your trading."

"No, as always, just jumping on opportunities as I see them."

"Ok, then," Greg said somewhat tentatively. "Then just keep knocking them out of the park."

The two men walked out of the court and to the showers. As Jack let cool water run over his head, he wondered if there was any truth to what Greg was saying. Was there a chance that the events over the past two months had influenced his trading? Studies showed that increased testosterone levels in traders consistently produced riskier and riskier trading patterns. But could the events of the past two months have increased his hormone levels? That seemed a stretch to Jack. However, maybe all the risks he was taking in his private life were enough to alter his tolerance for risk in general? He hated for anything to cause doubt in his trading decisions, but he would have to think twice about trades that fell outside of long-term value investing.

Greg Taylor started GDT Capital Group almost thirty-five years ago with five thousand dollars he borrowed from his father. He was known for being a ruthless bastard who lived in legal gray areas over the years, but he considered it all a part of a game; find a weakness in the system, exploit it, and make as much money as he could before congress or the SEC could plug the hole. By the time they caught on to what he was doing, he was already on to his next strategy. Always perfectly legal. But always pushing the limits. He was also known for making his employees rich.

There wasn't a single person at the firm who wasn't surprised when Greg announced his retirement. The consensus was that he would probably die at his desk and, even then, trade for at least a few more days. Sitting at the bar after getting washed up, Jack pried a little into Greg's future. "You going to miss it?" he asked.

Greg thought before answering, taking a sip of his twenty-year-old single malt Scotch. "Can you imagine swapping the adrenaline of managing more than a billion dollars for what, a cruise? Traveling through Italy? No, thank you."

"Then why leave?" Jack asked, quickly adding, "It's certainly none of my business, but you have a few years left before...."

"Before I become a liability to the fund?" Greg interjected.

"Well, I wasn't going to put it that way, but...."

"You don't need to know all my business, Jack. Let's say that circumstances beyond my control have led me to believe that this is the best decision for me, my family, and the fund."

Jack lifted his Old Fashioned to toast with Greg. "Well, I know you still have a couple of months to go, but I would like to take this opportunity to say a couple of things. I have learned a lot. I have made a lot. And I have had a great time along the way. I owe almost all of that to you."

Greg met his glass with a clink and took a sip. "Jack, it has been my pleasure."

"Well, please let me know if I can ever repay you."

"I will do that."

"Like, if you ever need bail money or... or if that beautiful wife of yours ever comes to her senses and decides to leave you and you need a place to stay...."

"Funny, Jack."

Jack smiled and gently slapped Greg on the shoulder as he stood up from the table.

"You leaving?" Greg asked. "I thought you might stick around and grab dinner with me."

Jack reached in to shake his hand. "I would love to, but Sarah is coming into the city for a night out."

Greg shook his hand without getting up from the table. "Maybe next time. Let's take advantage of the time we have, Jack, before Beth has me trapped on some god-awful cruise ship with a million little kids running around and days filled with tours of decrepit cities and boring old museums."

"Wow, Greg, had the whole private equity gig not worked out, you could have been a writer for travel guides."

"Goodbye, Jack. Enjoy your evening."

CHAPTER THIRTEEN

The next fantasy on Sarah's list was a big one: sleeping with a man other than Jack. Most people would consider the fantasies at the end of the list a much bigger deal, but not for Sarah. Taking this step, breaking this seal, was the one that carried with it the most emotion. She couldn't even contemplate the others until she had taken this step.

In the weeks that preceded their big night, Sarah discovered a talent that served her and Jack well in the bedroom. One night while making love, words spilled out of her mouth. She didn't plan it. It just happened. One minute they were quietly making love, and the next, she was putting words to the images that she had in her mind. It was the first real glimpse Jack got of the world Sarah had created. She would never have had the guts to speak the words for fear that it would upset or turn off Jack. But she could feel Jack's cock stiffen the second the words left her mouth. As it turns out, Jack was a fan. Did he want to see her fuck another man? Did he want to see another man's cock in her? Would he be threatened by how wet she got with someone else? Before

Jack and Sarah ever made it to Lux for the second time, they had already gotten miles and miles out of just thinking about what was to come.

Sarah didn't want to wear the same outfit as the first time they went, but she didn't want to go through another Brooke shopping experience either. After a bottle of wine and two hours of browsing online with Jack, she decided on a gorgeous, sexy black dress that was essentially see-through, would probably show most of her ass, and definitely would require double-sided tape to keep her nipples covered. Jack laughed to himself when Sarah picked it out. It was even skimpier than the first dress she wore. The one that "just wasn't her." *How quickly things change.*

In their quest to find a man to help fulfill her fantasy, they decided it would be best to opt for a single man, a bull, as Marcus described it. They could easily find a married man for the job, but that presented unnecessary variables. And the only way to find a single man at Lux was to go on a Friday night.

Sarah ran behind all day, trying to gather anything and everything they might need for the evening. She hadn't packed the first thing when her mother arrived to stay with Colin. The plan was for her to meet Jack at their favorite hotel after work so that he didn't have to trek out to the suburbs just to turn around and go back. His suitcase, of course, had been packed since the night before.

Juggling her bag, Jack's bag, and the hanging clothes bag, Sarah looked like a carnival act coming down the stairs.

"Sarah, dear, let me help you with that," her mother said.

"Thanks, Mom," Sarah said, handing her one of the bags.

Dropping the rest of the luggage by the door, Sarah turned to say goodbye to her son. "Where did Colin go?"

"He's in the living room."

Sarah walked back to give Colin a hug and a kiss along

with the obligatory "be nice for Granna." As she walked back into the foyer, Sarah realized that she had forgotten to pack a surprise she had bought for Jack. "Almost forgot something," she said as she turned to climb the stairs to her bedroom. A couple of minutes later, coming back down with a shopping bag in hand, Sarah saw her mother unzipping her hanging clothes bag.

"Mom, don't!"

Sarah's mother went wide-eyed as she pulled out the skimpy black dress. She took a couple of steps backward and sat on a chair as if her legs weren't going to hold her much longer. Sarah placed the shopping bag on a side table and walked over to take the dress from her mother. Putting it back, she said, "Mom, I don't want to discuss this."

"Sarah, I just wanted to see what you were wearing tonight," she said on the verge of tears. "I don't even know what to say about...this," she said as if the word was dirty as it left her mouth. *This.*

"And that is why I don't want to discuss it."

Sarah turned around and walked back to lay the clothing bag over her other luggage.

"Are you having an affair?" her mother asked.

"Mom, no!"

"Please just be honest with me. Are you cheating on Jack?"

Sarah dropped her head and walked into the living room to sit down.

"Honey, you may not want to discuss it, but I know how hard marriage can be. I'm not judging you."

"Mom, I'm not having an affair. Do you think I would bring Jack's suitcase with me to have an affair?"

"If you had asked me yesterday, I would have said no. But this?" she said, pointing to the hanging clothes bag.

"Mom, Jack and I are in a good place, I promise."

Sarah's mom looked over at the bag on the side table. "I'm almost afraid to ask what's in there," she said, pointing to the bag.

Sarah froze. "Mom, don't you dare."

Her mother hesitated only a second before she dashed to the side table, reached into the bag, and pulled out a box. Sarah almost tripped over the couch trying to stop her, but the damage had been done by the time she ripped the box from her mother's hands. A glimpse was all it took for her to see that the box contained a large, black vibrator with "Lifelike" printed across the box in giant letters.

Sarah's mother returned to her chair, sat down, and began to cry.

"Mom, please don't do this," Sarah pleaded.

"Lifelike, Sarah?" she said, wiping tears from her eyes. "I don't know whose life they're talking about because I've never seen anything like that in *my* life."

"Okay, enough," Sarah said as she placed the bag next to the luggage.

Sarah's mom sat for a moment in silence. "What happened to my sweet little girl?" she asked.

"God, Mom, please. It's just sex. Between a husband and wife," she added, knowing that wasn't entirely true. "I refuse to go down this road with you to explain anything about my sex life."

Sarah walked over and hugged her mom's head into her stomach. They remained there for several minutes until there was a knock at the door.

"Mrs. Williams?" Yuri asked through the cracked door.

"Hey, Yuri, I'm almost ready."

Looking at the two women hugging, he could tell Sarah's mother was upset. "I'm sorry to interrupt. I will grab the bags and wait in the car," Yuri said with a thick Russian accent.

"Leave the shopping bag, Yuri."

"Yes, ma'am," he said as he slowly retreated with the other bags.

Sarah gave her mother a gentle squeeze before backing away to look at her. "Mom, I'm sorry to have upset you, but I need you to know something. Jack and I are in a good place. A really good place. Please don't make more out of this than it is? Okay?"

Sarah's mother wiped away the tears under her eyes and stood up. "I don't understand any of this, Sarah."

"Mom, please just trust me?"

"There is something not right here, and I don't know what it is," she said as she continuously shook her head back and forth. "But I guess my only choice is to take you at your word."

"Thank you. That's all I'm asking." Sarah took her hand and wiped tears off her mother's face. "Are you okay to stay with Colin?"

"While you are gallivanting around the city doing God knows what with God knows whom?"

"Mom?"

Her mother waited a moment before answering. "I'll be fine. He'll be fine."

Sarah stepped in close and hugged her. "Thank you, Mom. I love you."

"I love you, too."

Sarah turned and headed to the door. She wanted to turn around and say something to her mother, but no words came to her. Instead, she grabbed the shopping bag and made her exit without looking back.

CHAPTER FOURTEEN

*J*ack was sitting on the end of their hotel bed, holding the box with the enormous "Lifelike" dildo. Half laughing, half cringing, he said, "I would like to have seen her face."

"No, you wouldn't. It was the most terrible combination of disgust and disapproval and disappointment. I think it was the only time in my life that I was happy that my father wasn't alive," she said. "I will never be able to see it again without thinking about Mom's face."

"You think they'll let you return a used dildo?"

"I'm sure it's fine if it's never been opened. So, can you please stop playing with it? Please?"

Jack set the giant silicone phallus on the nightstand. "And if you don't mind me asking, what was your thinking behind buying this?"

"I was thinking that if we couldn't find someone tonight to help with the fantasy, we could simulate it with more than words when we got back to the room."

"And why do you think we will have a hard time finding someone this evening?"

"I don't know. I guess I don't know what to expect." She sat down next to him on the bed and leaned her head against his shoulder. "Now, with all of the nonsense with my mom, I'm not sure that I'm in the right headspace for any of it."

"Oh no, you don't," Jack said, lifting her off the bed by her hand and guiding her towards the shower. "We've been planning this night for a long time."

Sarah stopped short of the bathroom and turned around. "Jack, every time I look at myself in that dress, it will remind me of that look in my mom's eyes."

Jack spun her around again and gave a gentle nudge towards the bathroom. "I'll make you a deal; you can take it off as soon as we get to the club."

"Funny."

---

*E*verything about their second visit to Lux was different from the first. Sarah was excited to get inside and dance rather than being so scared that she wanted to throw up. Jack quietly presented his driver's license at the front desk rather than scream his name. And once they made it inside, they realized just how different the club was on nights that allowed single men. Because they were everywhere.

Walking through the doors into the main part of the club, Sarah stopped in her tracks. "Drink," she said quickly, overwhelmed by the ratio of men to women.

"Definitely," Jack replied, taking her by the hand and guiding her to the bar. "26544," Jack said to the bartender. "I'll have two vodka sodas...."

"One with lemon, one plain?" the bartender said, interrupting Jack before he could finish.

Jack smiled. "You got it, thanks."

"Welcome back. I thought we might have lost you two," the bartender said with a smile.

"Why do you say that?"

"In my experience, this place either clicks with you or doesn't. I usually see people every weekend for the first couple of months when it does. When it doesn't, I generally don't see them again." He handed the drinks over to Jack with a slight grin.

"So, where does that leave us?" Jack asked.

"Well, there are several possible scenarios, but I guess your wife either had a gun to your head to stay away or...she has a gun to your head tonight to come back."

Jack laughed. "Nope, everyone came voluntarily." He grabbed the drinks. "Thanks."

"You are most welcome," the bartender said.

Jack turned to Sarah and smiled. "You okay?"

"This is a lot to take in, Jack."

"No worries. Let's finish our drink, go dance, and if it happens, it happens. Deal?"

"Deal."

Jack guided her to a table and took a seat. "Besides, if it doesn't work out, we always have Captain Lifelike waiting for us back at the Aspect East Village Hotel!" Jack belted out the hotel's name in the same tone as the television announcer in their commercials.

"Aspect East?" came a voice from the table next to them.

Jack turned to find an attractive African American man, possibly in his mid-forties. "I'm sorry," Jack said. "I didn't catch what you asked. What did you say about the Aspect East?"

The man laughed. "I didn't mean to eavesdrop, but I thought I heard you talking about the Aspect East. You've heard of it?"

"Absolutely. It's rapidly becoming our favorite," Jack said. "You've stayed there before?"

The man smiled. "I've been there a few times."

Jack stood and extended his hand. "I'm Jack, and this is my wife, Sarah."

The man stood up and shook both of their hands. "Nice to meet you. People call me CJ."

"No name, just CJ?" Jack asked with a smile.

"Just CJ until I know you better, Jack," he said as he winked at Sarah. "Do you mind if I join you?"

"Not at all," Jack said, pulling a chair out from the table.

"Is this your first time here?" CJ asked.

"No, we've been here once before," Sarah said.

"But first time dealing with single men?"

"Yes, that is true. Does it show?" Jack asked.

"A little. You'll see it too once you've been around a little while." CJ finished his drink and placed his glass on the table. "Anyone care for some champagne?" he asked, looking around the table.

"I would love some," Jack said.

"Sarah?" CJ asked. "How about you, love?"

"That would be great, thanks."

CJ pushed his chair back and stood up. Once he got the bartender's attention, he held up three fingers. The bartender nodded without expression and disappeared into a back room. Moments later, he emerged with an ice bucket, a bottle of champagne, and three champagne flutes.

"Much appreciated, Preston," CJ said, taking the champagne bottle. "So, what shall we toast to?" CJ asked as he unwrapped the foil.

"No idea," Jack asked. "Sarah? Suggestions?"

"I don't have a clue," Sarah said.

CJ began to unwrap the wire cage from the bottle. "Okay, you two are overthinking it. I got this." With a napkin over the top of the bottle, and a gentle twist or two, the cork popped out into CJ's hand. He carefully poured out three glasses of champagne and placed the bottle back on ice. Holding his glass up to meet theirs, he said, "To finding what we are each looking for."

Sarah let out a shallow laugh as she clinked glasses and took a sip of champagne. "What are we all looking for?" she asked.

"Ah, it is different for everyone, Sarah," CJ said with a smile.

"And what makes you think we are looking for something?" Sarah asked.

Taking a sip of champagne, CJ leaned back in his chair with a grin. "Everyone who steps foot through that door is looking for something."

"Oh really," she replied. "And when you stepped through the door tonight, what were *you* looking for?"

CJ took another sip of champagne, placed the glass on the table, and leaned close to Sarah. "What was *I* looking for?" he asked.

Sarah took a sip of her champagne, placed her glass on the table, and leaned close to CJ. "Yes, what were *you* looking for?"

CJ smiled and waited a moment, looking into Sarah's eyes. Finally, he said, "*I* was looking for *you*."

Sarah laughed as she leaned back in her chair. "Oh. My. God. CJ, let me ask you, are all the single men here tonight this bad?"

CJ drew his hands to his chest and made a pained face like he was offended. "No way, I'm way worse than most," he said. "Besides," he said, leaning in to pick up his drink. "I'm not a single man tonight."

Sarah cocked her head sideways. "So, where is your wife?"

Looking down at his ringless finger, she added, "Or girlfriend?"

"She's a friend from Chicago. Sometimes we play together when she's in town, but at the moment, she is in the back playing with others."

"Play together?" Jack asked.

"Well, we wingman for one another. She is a fan of the ladies."

"And you? What are you a fan of?" Sarah chimed in.

"I'm a fan of helping white women check a box," CJ said. "I'm a helper. I like to help people," he said with a smile.

"Someone's first black man?" Sarah inquired.

"That or a woman's first large...."

"Okay, we get the picture," Sarah interrupted. "And no love for the black women?"

"Well. I love black women, but they generally don't come to a club like this looking for their first time with a black man." CJ filled each of their glasses with more champagne. "If a black woman comes here looking to check a box, she will typically be looking for a woman, a couple, or possibly a white guy."

"Interesting," Sarah said.

"And I should add that when I say someone comes here looking for something, whether it is white or black or Asian or Hispanic or male or female, what I should be saying is that they are generally looking for different. Different from what they have at home."

Jack reached out, took Sarah's hand, and gave it a gentle squeeze. "I need to run to the bathroom. Do you want to join me, or are you okay with CJ?"

"I'm good right here, thanks."

Standing up, Jack turned and faced CJ across the table. "I trust you'll keep an eye on my bride while I am gone?"

CJ raised his glass in Jack's direction. "I will guard her

with my life." Lifting the almost empty bottle of champagne, he split what remained between the glasses. "One more?" he asked Sarah, holding the empty bottle upside down.

"Sure," she said. "Why not?"

CJ stood up and caught the bartender's eye while holding up the empty champagne bottle. Once again, expressionless, the bartender nodded and disappeared into a back room.

"So, how long have you two been married?" CJ asked.

Before Sarah could answer, someone over her shoulder responded for her. "About eight years," came the familiar voice.

Sarah's mind raced to put a face or a name with the voice. While Sarah struggled to make the connection, she continued to stare straight ahead without moving.

When CJ saw that Sarah was on the verge of panic, he stood up and offered the stranger his hand. "Hi, I'm CJ."

"Hello, CJ," the familiar voice said. "I'm Greg, Sarah's husband's boss."

CHAPTER FIFTEEN

"Hello, Mr. Taylor," Sarah managed to force out of her mouth without turning around.

"Call me Greg, please," he said as he walked around the table into Sarah's view. He couldn't help but glance down at what little there was of Sarah's dress. "I think things are a little too casual here to be calling anyone mister."

Sarah instinctively did her best to cover what she could of her body with her arms and legs as she stared down at her drink.

"Is Jack here with you, or is it just you and CJ this evening?" Greg asked.

"Jack is in the restroom," she said.

Greg looked at CJ and asked, "Do you mind if I join you for a few minutes? I feel I should at least say hello to Jack."

CJ looked across at Sarah. "That would be a question for the lady as this is their table."

Sarah looked up briefly to make eye contact. "Of course, please."

As Greg was helping himself to a chair, the bartender

arrived with the bottle of champagne. "Would you like another glass?" the bartender asked, looking at CJ.

Greg looked over at Sarah. "If it is okay with Sarah, I would love one."

Without looking up, Sarah said, "Actually, it's CJ's champagne."

Greg looked over at CJ with raised eyebrows. "CJ?"

Looking at Sarah, CJ could tell that having drinks with this man was about the last thing she wanted to do, but she had allowed him to sit. Who was he to say no to a drink? "Yes, certainly."

Returning from the bathroom, Jack could see three men around Sarah from across the room. Instantly he was mad at himself for leaving her alone. In a sex club. On single men's night. Yet his anger quickly faded as he realized that one of the men was CJ, the other was the bartender, and a third man, was seated with his back to Jack. When Sarah noticed Jack walking up, her face made it clear that she wanted to be anywhere but here.

Greg noticed Sarah looking over his shoulder. He stood up and turned to greet Jack with an enormous smile. "Hello, Jack."

Jack's heart began to beat out of his chest. "Mr. Taylor? What are you doing here?"

"Well, I don't know, Jack. I would assume the same thing everyone is doing here."

Jack stumbled up to the table and managed to sit, though he came close to missing the chair altogether. "I just mean, what are you doing here?" Jack asked again.

Greg took a sip of champagne. "I've been a member of this club since Studio Fifty-Four was a thing. So, I believe the better question is, what are you doing here?"

Jack looked across the table at Sarah and then at CJ.

Finally, he looked back at Greg. "Honestly, sir, I don't really know how to answer that question."

"Well, for whatever reason you are here, I would appreciate it if you would stop calling me Mr. Taylor or sir."

"Yes, sir," Jack said without thinking. "I mean, Greg."

What followed was probably only ten seconds of silence, but it felt like eternity for most of them. When a new song started, CJ turned to Sarah. "Do you like to dance?"

"Excuse me?" Sarah asked, looking back at CJ.

"Do you like to dance?"

"I love it," she said, looking back at Jack.

CJ turned to Jack. "Do you mind if I take Sarah out on the dance floor and leave you two gentlemen to talk?"

"Sure, that's fine," Jack said, looking back at Sarah. "If you're okay with it."

Sarah forced a smile, stood up, and kissed Jack. Leaning into his ear and squeezing his hand, she whispered, "Of all the gin joints...."

CJ stood up, took Sarah by the hand, and headed for the dance floor.

Jack and Greg sat without talking for almost twenty seconds before Greg broke the silence. "We don't need to make this weird, Jack."

Jack looked out on the dancefloor as his wife, half-naked, danced with a man he didn't know while sitting next to his boss in a sex club. "Greg, I honestly can't imagine how this could get any weirder."

"Oh, it can. Trust me."

"I'm afraid even to consider it." He took a sip of his champagne and tried not to let his imagination run away with him.

"I like pain, Jack," Greg said matter-of-factly.

Jack spit champagne out, covering most of the table.

"I told you it could get weirder," Greg said.

Jack put his glass down and looked over at Greg. "Why would you tell me that?"

"I'm just trying to get you to relax. There isn't a soul in this club racing home in the afternoon excited to knock out a little missionary with their spouse of twenty years. Not one."

"And if you don't mind me asking, is Beth here with you?"

Greg smiled. "She normally would be, but Fridays I come alone. Beth is not a fan of pain, giving or receiving, but she allows me a little freedom in satisfying my particular kink."

"Pain?"

"Well, there is an element of pain. But ultimately, it's about submission and giving complete control to another human being."

"Are you talking about bondage?"

"I don't think we need to get into the details, but I thought telling you this much might put you at ease regarding your wife's fantasy to sleep with a black man."

Jack snapped around to look at Greg. "Who said Sarah had a fantasy to sleep with a black man?"

"Oh, Jack, don't take offense. It was a guess, and based on your response, I believe an accurate one. Trust me, Beth and I have been members of this club for almost as long as you've been alive. You would have to work really, really hard to surprise me."

Watching CJ dance with Sarah made Jack sad that Greg had derailed their evening. CJ appeared to be teaching Sarah some dance steps that she was picking up like a natural.

"Jack?" Greg said for the second time.

"I'm sorry. Just trying to wrap my brain around how different the two clubs are that we belong to: a squash club and a sex club."

Greg laughed. "I believe that likely makes three clubs."

"Three?" Jack asked, a bit confused.

"The Mile High Club," Greg said with a smile.

"Actually," Jack said. "We don't belong to that one."

"So, you skipped right over the easy one and went straight for the sex club, eh?" Greg laughed. "I guess that's one way to go."

"I guess," Jack said as he watched Sarah dance.

Greg smiled and lifted his glass. "Well, we'll have to work on that."

Opening the door to the suite, Jack was thinking about all the ways their evening might have ended. Greg's presence had killed the mood for Sarah. CJ was clearly disappointed when they left, but he promised them that they would cross paths again soon. Jack had wanted to ask him for his contact information, but it seemed awkward. They opted instead for a handshake and a gentle kiss on the lips for Sarah.

Walking into the suite, they found a room service cart in their living room with a giant bowl full of strawberries placed next to an ice bucket and champagne on it. Jack looked back at Sarah. "Is this your doing?"

"No, I swear. I wish I had thought of it."

Jack walked over to the cart and picked up the card on the table. It was from the general manager of the hotel. It read:

"For two of our favorite guests at the Aspect East Village Hotel. I hope you have time to relax and enjoy the champagne, the strawberries, and the chocolate. If there is anything I can do to make your visit special, please don't hesitate to call."

It was a typed message but attributed to the general manager, and it even listed his phone number at the bottom.

"Where are the chocolates?" Sarah asked. "That would make my night."

Jack shook his head. "Sarah," he said. "Can you look up

the GM for me of this hotel? See if his picture is on the website?"

"What's his name?" Sarah asked.

"Just search for the hotel online, and you tell me."

Sarah pulled out her phone and started to search. After about a minute, she said, "Calvin Johnson."

"Is there a picture?" Jack asked.

"One second," she said.

Jack could see the second she found one because she lowered her phone and looked up at him with her eyes and mouth wide open. "CJ? Are you freaking kidding me?"

Jack just smiled and ate a strawberry. "So, a question for you."

"What's that?"

Holding up the card, he said, "Am I calling room service and ordering the chocolate?"

CHAPTER SIXTEEN

Jack opened the door to find CJ holding a bottle of champagne and a plate of chocolates.

"Mr. Williams, I understand that something was missing from your earlier room service delivery?" CJ said in an overly formal voice.

"So it would appear," Jack said as he used his hand to gesture into the suite. "Come in."

Sarah immediately walked over and kissed CJ on the cheek. "General manager of our favorite hotel? What are the odds?"

"And yet, here I am," CJ replied.

"Yes, here you are," Sarah said with a smile.

Jack retrieved a champagne flute from the cart and poured CJ a glass. "I guess the third glass should have been a clue?"

"Three glasses? I'm sure that must have been a fluke," CJ said with a grin.

"Again, what are the odds?" Jack laughed. "Should have played the lottery today." Jack gestured for CJ to take a seat in the living area.

"If you will excuse me, gentlemen, I was just about to change out of this dress," Sarah said as she walked back towards the bedroom.

"So," CJ said, "your boss said you two have been married for eight years?"

"I missed that conversation, but yes," Jack replied.

"And how long have you and Sarah been in the lifestyle?"

"Lifestyle?" Jack asked while pouring three glasses of champagne.

CJ leaned forward in his chair. "That long, huh?"

Jack looked up at CJ with a blank stare as he handed him a glass of champagne and sat down on the couch across from him. "I'm sorry, I don't understand what you mean."

"How long have you and your wife been sleeping with other people?" CJ asked, taking a sip of champagne.

"Oh," Jack said. "Never."

CJ let out a soft whistle, placed his champagne on the coffee table, and stood up. "I am so sorry. I completely misread the situation."

Sarah walked out of the bedroom wearing nothing but Jack's white button-down as he finished his statement.

Jack looked over at CJ and took a sip of champagne. "No, CJ. I don't think you did."

Sarah walked over to the couch, sat crossed legged next to Jack, and picked up a glass of her own.

CJ cocked his head a little sideways. "Seriously?" he asked, looking back and forth between them.

"Seriously, what?" Sarah asked.

"He's asking if we seriously want him to check your box," Jack said.

"Cute, Jack," Sarah said, hitting him on the arm. She looked up at CJ. "You ok?"

CJ just shook his head. "I'm sorry, I just want to make sure we are all on the same page."

Sarah stood up and placed her champagne glass on the table. "How about we check off the 'dance with another man in front of my husband box' and see where that leads?" Sarah asked. "Would that clear things up for you?"

CJ smiled and held out his hand. "I think that makes it clear enough."

Sarah took his hand and led him to an open area in the room. She gently wrapped both arms around his waist, tucked her head against his chest, and began slow dancing to an unheard song. "Jack, can you find us a little music, please?" she asked.

"Sure," he said.

Jack made his way to the entertainment panel and selected a slow song.

After a few minutes, CJ's hands slowly made their way down to Sarah's ass. Jack walked around the room, turning off most of the lights, leaving just enough for him to see them.

"Babe, you ok?" Sarah asked as he took a seat in a chair not far from the dancing.

"I'm good," he said.

Sarah reached her hand up behind CJ's neck and pulled him down to kiss her. After gently kissing her, he pulled away and continued to dance. A moment later, Sarah reached up and kissed him again. Though it was a bit longer the second time, CJ pulled away again. Finally, Sarah stopped dancing, reached up with both hands, and pulled him down for a kiss he would not leave.

"Jack, we still good?" she asked.

"Sarah, I'm fine. I promise that if at any point I'm uncomfortable, you will be the first to know," he said. "Now, focus on CJ."

Sarah began to unbutton his shirt. When it fell to the floor, CJ lifted Sarah in his arms and began to walk toward the bedroom. When he got halfway there, he stopped and looked back at Jack, who hadn't moved. "You coming?"

"I was thinking about giving you two a head start," Jack replied.

CJ looked down at Sarah, waiting to see how she felt about that.

"I'd feel a lot better if you were there the whole time, Jack," she said in a tone that made it clear that there was no other option.

Jack stood up and walked towards the bedroom. As he passed them, he leaned in and kissed Sarah. "Brooke was right," he said.

"About what?" she asked.

"You are one hot momma," he said, kissing her once more before walking into the bedroom and sitting next to the bed.

CJ followed behind him and gently laid Sarah in the middle of the bed. He smiled down at her as he kicked off his shoes and socks. When he began to unbuckle his pants, Jack threw a box of condoms on the bed by Sarah. She grabbed the box and held it up to CJ.

CJ smiled and pulled a condom out of his pocket. "Have condom. Will travel."

Sarah laughed. "You always walk around with condoms in your pocket?"

"I generally need to," CJ replied as he stepped out of his pants and underwear.

"Holy shit!" Sarah said when she saw the size of his cock. "Are you kidding me?"

"Um...Sarah?" Jack asked.

"Yeah?" she replied.

"Are you thinking what I'm thinking?"

"I'm thinking many things right now, Jack, but I'm not in the mood to play a guessing game."

"I'm thinking it was lifelike after all."

Sarah just stared at CJ's cock. "That was definitely one of the things I was thinking." She reached out, grabbed him with two hands, and pulled him to the side of the bed. CJ stepped forward as she pulled.

"Careful," he said. "Big doesn't mean durable."

"I'm sorry," Sarah said, releasing only one hand. She used the other hand to lead him up onto the bed. With CJ centered in the bed, Sarah climbed up to his far side so as not to block Jack's view. She stroked him a couple of times before making a weird face. "Jack, come sit over here," she said, pointing to the chair behind her.

"Really?" he asked.

"Yes, really," she replied. "I can't do this with my left hand."

Jack laughed. "Ok then."

As Jack walked to the other side of the bed, Sarah climbed over CJ's legs without releasing his cock. She passed it from her left hand to her right hand with the grace of a Jamaican four-by-one-hundred track star passing a baton. Sitting crossed-legged, Sarah sat stroking CJ with a look of disbelief. She looked up and made eye contact with Jack. She just smiled and shook her head. Jack just shrugged his shoulders as if to say, "I can't believe this."

In one quick motion, Sarah flipped up on her knees and leaned over CJ's cock. With a smile at Jack and a quick curl of her hair behind her ear, she approached CJ's cock with her mouth. Tentatively, Sarah licked it two or three times. Then she looked up at CJ.

"It's okay," he said. "You don't have to."

"Fuck that," she said. Sarah seemed to study the situation for a moment, took a quick breath, and stuck as much of it in her mouth as she could—which wasn't far.

"That feels good," CJ said.

Sarah pulled her head up, gasped for air, and gave CJ a dirty look.

"Seriously, it feels good," he said.

Sarah looked at his cock as if she were someone on the cliffs high above the water, trying to get the courage to jump. After a few seconds, she drove her mouth down over his cock. Two or three thrusts later, she gagged and lifted her head. With tears forming in her eyes and saliva dripping from her mouth, CJ sat up and wiped the tears from her eyes.

"Gold star for effort, but that's enough," CJ said. He gently guided her onto her back in the middle of the bed. Positioning himself between her legs, he stroked himself a couple of times with one hand and slipped a finger in Sarah with another. "Damn," he said. "I normally would suggest a lot of lube, but...."

"Jack, come here, please," Sarah said. "Right here. Just like with Marcus."

"Hang on a second," CJ said while he slowly stroked himself. "I thought this was going be a first?"

"It is," Jack said. "Marcus checked an oral box."

"Got it," CJ said with a smile. "I'm not complaining either way." Opening the condom wrapper with his teeth, CJ quickly had the condom in hand and around his cock in no time. He lifted Sarah's legs a little into the air and positioned himself between them. He stroked his cock a couple more times before laying it over her vagina and part of her stomach.

Sarah swallowed hard. "Jack, are we still good?" she asked.

Jack just sat there staring.

"Jack?"

"Yes," he finally said. "I'm good if you are."

When she didn't immediately answer, CJ asked her, "Are *you* good?"

"Yes, I'm good," she said.

With that, CJ backed far enough away from Sarah that he

could rub the head of his cock on her clit, which he did for a while. "Everyone still okay?" he asked.

"Yes," they answered together.

CJ pulled back a little bit further and began barely rubbing the edge of the lips of Sarah's vagina. It didn't take long for Sarah to rub herself against him. After a moment, CJ held his cock perfectly still as Sarah thrust herself up and down and slowly forward. She squeezed Jack's hands as small moans began to leave her lips.

CJ lifted his erection and moved closer to Sarah. "You okay?" he asked Sarah.

"Jack?" she asked.

"I'm good," he said.

Sarah looked up at CJ and nodded.

CJ rubbed the tip of his cock just inside Sarah's lips. Sarah gently pulsed up and down. When CJ moved closer, the head of his cock pressed just enough to slip part of the way inside her. CJ stopped moving.

"It's okay. Just go slow," she said.

CJ began to barely rock back and forth, a fraction of an inch at most. As the head of his cock finally made it completely inside her, she let out a moan.

"Holy shit," she said, digging her fingernails into the side of his leg.

As CJ continued to rock back and forth, his stroke got incrementally deeper.

"Okay, okay, give me a second," Sarah asked.

"Just breathe," CJ said with a smile. "Women have babies every day. And this doesn't even compare."

"Yes, but they give those women drugs," Sarah replied.

CJ stopped the back-and-forth motion and gently pressed himself as deep as he could. Sarah let out a soft moan and pushed back against him. "Ok, it's too much," she said as she quickly pulled away from him. "Rollover," she instructed.

CJ did as he was asked and flipped on his back. Sarah quickly climbed above him and gently lowered herself down his shaft. It only took a minute or two, but she was finally able to take all of him. She grabbed his hands and moved them from her hips to her breasts.

"Fuck," she said as she began a breathing pattern Jack had heard many times before. Thrusting. Breathing. Thrusting. Not breathing. Thrusting. Orgasm.

Sarah collapsed onto CJ's chest.

"Box checked," Sarah said with a little laugh. "And I mean, seriously fucking checked."

CJ, with his still hard erection, began to gently thrust up into her.

"Give me a second," Sarah said. She climbed off of CJ and stood by the bed. "Jack, I need you naked right there," she said, pointing to a space on the bed just in front of the headboard. "And in a second, I'm going to need you, right there," Sarah said to CJ as she pointed to the foot of the bed.

Jack was naked, centered on the bed, leaning back against the headboard in a flash. Sarah smiled at Jack as she crawled up on the bed and took him into her mouth. She patted her ass, inviting CJ to come and take her from behind.

As CJ entered her, she released Jack's cock and took a big breath.

"Gentle," she said.

"I'm always gentle," CJ protested.

"There's nothing gentle about that thing," Sarah said before taking Jack back into her mouth.

CJ barely put more than the head of his cock in Sarah. But in no time, she was the one who began to lengthen the stride. She was pushing back against him with each thrust. Small moans started to come out of her as CJ thrust quicker and deeper. Jack tried to hold off, but he could tell Sarah was about to come again, and there was no chance he would make it through that.

Sarah pulled Jack's cock out of her mouth as she gasped to breathe. With her ass high in the air, she buried her head into Jack just next to his cock. She stroked his cock while he came until her muscle contractions halted all movement.

CJ stopped.

"Don't stop," Sarah instructed. "Please, I want you to come."

CJ started to thrust again, slower in pace but with more force. Sarah wrapped her arms around Jack and let little moans escape her lips with every thrust. Jack rubbed her back, trying not to distract CJ by making eye contact. When the moaning reached a point that Jack could no longer tell if they were pleasure or pain, he asked her if she was ok.

"Uh-huh," she replied.

"Are you sure?"

"Uh-huh," she confirmed.

About a minute later, CJ let out a groan as he came.

Sarah took a deep breath and leaned forward, pulling away from CJ. She kissed Jack's stomach, rolled over beside him, and started to laugh.

"What's so funny," Jack asked.

"When I am filling out my Yelp review tomorrow for the hotel, remind me to focus on the incredible room service."

CHAPTER SEVENTEEN

Walking into the office on Monday morning was stressful for Jack. Not only had his boss expressed concerns about the risks he was taking in his trading life, but he also happened to run into him at a sex club. And that wasn't even touching on the whole bondage discussion. If nothing else, it would all make for an interesting day.

"Morning, Kathy," he said as he entered his office.

"Good morning, Mr. Williams," she replied, handing him a stack of papers. "Dr. Lieberman called to confirm the investment in the Traveleru startup. Mr. Oliver called concerned about some potential tax issues. And Mr. Taylor asked that I schedule some time with him this morning for you two to speak."

Jack looked up at Kathy. "Taylor? How did he sound?"

"Sounded normal to me. Is there something I should be concerned with?"

"No, Kathy, everything is fine. I have a couple of things I needed to speak with him about, but I didn't expect him to address them this quickly."

"Well, I took the liberty of sneaking thirty minutes after your ten o'clock. Hopefully, that will be enough time."

"Perfect. Thank you."

Jack struggled to concentrate through his morning meetings. All he could think about was Mr. Taylor strapped to a table being spanked by some over-the-top stereotypical tiny Asian woman. And what exactly did he want to talk about that was so urgent?

When the appointed hour came, and Jack walked into Mr. Taylor's office, Greg stood up from his chair with a grin and offered Jack his hand. "Shut the door, Jack. We need to chat."

"Well, that sounds ominous," Jack said as he shut the door.

"No worries, Jack. Take a seat."

Jack sat in front of the desk and forced himself to make eye contact with Greg.

"I wanted to have a quick chat about a few things. First of all, even without regard to club policy, I assume I can count on your discretion regarding my private life?"

"Greg, I would never tell a soul about you being there or what you shared with me."

"Well, full disclosure, I did tell Beth that I ran into you and Sarah at the club. I was concerned that if I didn't warn her first, she might have a heart attack if she saw you there."

Jack let out a small groan at the thought of seeing Beth at the next company gathering or at the club itself, for that matter. "And how did she take that information?"

"Typical woman. She asked about Sarah's dress. Oh, and about the shoes, of course."

Jack laughed. "No mention or shock about us being at the club?"

"None."

"Okay then."

"And the second thing is this: I am turning over a new

account to you. Viktor Dmitrievich Kozlov. It's a fifty-million-dollar deal, Jack."

Jack had never heard of the client, but he immediately refused. "Greg, I was serious when I said I would never tell anyone. I feel like you are trying to buy my silence."

"Jack, I am not trying to buy you off. I'm a month or so away from retiring. Viktor has a great track record in the wheat business and a terrible one with investments. It makes sense for the firm to start him with whoever will handle the account long-term. And I think that should be you."

"Fifty million dollars is enough to make anyone a little paranoid."

"He will be fine. Just do your best to be consistent and trustworthy and don't do anything that has the slightest chance of making him feel like he's getting screwed again."

Jack still felt uncomfortable with the situation, but there was nothing he could do about it.

"Which brings me to my last point," Greg said with a grin. "I need you to fly out to Seattle this Friday to meet him for dinner. Represent the firm. Let him put a face to the name. Do what you do best. Reassure him that there is no better place to invest his money than with GDT Capital."

Jack was excited about the prospects, but this last-minute trip would throw a wrench into his weekend plans with Sarah.

"Oh, one last thing. Why don't you take one of the company jets?" he asked. "And bring Sarah along to keep you company."

CHAPTER EIGHTEEN

Sarah could see Teterboro Airport off in the distance as the limo pulled off of Route Seventeen. She grabbed Jack by the sleeve. "Are you sure this is okay with Mr. Taylor?"

Jack smiled. "We wouldn't get through the security gate if this wasn't okay with Greg," he reassured her.

"Well, for the record, we aren't through the gate yet."

Jack smiled and rubbed her leg.

"It just seems a little coincidental that we run into him at the club, and a week later, he suggests that you take me with you to a business dinner on the other side of the country."

"Nothing coincidental about it," Jack said.

The limo hadn't come to a complete stop when the security guard raised the gate and waved them through. Jack turned and smiled at Sarah. Driving out onto the tarmac, Yuri swung the limo around and brought it to a stop right beside the plane. Jack turned to Sarah before opening the door. "If you're uncomfortable with this, I can ask Yuri to drive you back home."

"Screw that. We're through the gate," Sarah said with a

playful grin. "Besides, I have always wanted to fly on a small jet like this...pretend I'm rich and famous."

"You are rich."

"You know what I mean."

"Well then, you will be happy to know that this is the jet of choice for those who are rich *and famous*," Jack said with a silly look on his face.

"What does that mean?"

"It's a G5, baby."

"Well, not sure what that means, but I see it excites you. That's good enough for me," Sarah said.

The Director of Flight Operations for GDT Capital greeted them as they stepped out of the limo. "Mr. Williams, always good to see you."

"Hey, Ben, this is my wife, Sarah. Sarah, this is Ben Thompson. He runs the place."

"Sarah, nice to meet you," Ben said, gesturing towards the aircraft. "The flight crew is already on board, though no flight attendants will be joining you this afternoon." Ben paused for a moment as he made eye contact with Jack. "Per Mr. Taylor's instructions."

All Jack could do was smile as Sarah quickly glanced at him.

"No worries, Ben. I'm sure we'll be fine," Jack replied.

He had flown countless times on this plane, but never without a flight attendant. Jack knew very well why Greg had made the request. It was the same reason he had asked Sarah to wear a skirt. There was another club to join. He assumed Ben knew as well, which would explain the awkward silence that followed.

Yuri loaded their bags onto the jet as Jack and Sarah climbed aboard. Ben followed close behind and stood just behind the bulkhead. Leaning into the plane and gesturing forward, he said,

"Jack, Sarah, this is Captain Madeline Turner on the left and First Officer Chad Stewart on the right." Ben paused for a second as Jack and Sarah stepped forward. "Maddie, Chad, these are your passengers for the weekend, Jack and Sarah Williams."

"Nice to meet you both," Maddie said, looking over her shoulder. "Beautiful day to fly."

Chad just smiled, waved, and returned his focus to the cockpit.

Sarah leaned her head forward so she could see the controls better. "Good Lord, I expected to see a bunch of switches and dials, but this looks like a giant video game. How in the world did you ever learn to fly it?"

"Uncle Sam paid a lot of money for us to learn to fly planes many times more complex than these," Maddie said. "Air Force, twelve years."

"And you, Chad?" Sarah inquired.

"I did eight in the Navy," he replied.

Sarah shook her head. "Impressive all the same. I'm not sure there would ever be enough years for me to learn all of this."

"It's not that bad," Maddie said. "Especially when you don't have to worry about someone shooting at you."

Sarah laughed. "Well, fingers crossed." She turned and walked back into the cabin.

Ben shook Jack's hand. "Have a great trip," he said as he turned to walk down the stairs.

Sarah gestured to the door. "Jack, do you need to help with that?"

Jack smiled. "Nope, I think he's got it."

With the press of a button, the stairs began to rise and pull into place. Ben waved from the far side of the closing door.

From the cockpit, the captain called out to Jack. "Mr.

Williams, I understand you are familiar with the aircraft and its amenities?"

"I am."

"Great. Then if you both will grab a seat, we will go ahead and get underway. Unless you need us for something, we will see you in Seattle."

Sarah gave Jack a dirty look. "No flight attendant?"

"Nope," Jack replied.

"Wear a skirt?"

"Yes, ma'am."

"See you in Seattle?" Sarah sat down in the closest seat and buckled in. "They know exactly what you plan to do back here."

"No doubt," Jack said, sitting in a seat facing Sarah. "Doesn't it feel wrong?" he continued with a grin.

"Don't wear that out, Jack. Besides, joining the Mile High Club was never one of my fantasies." She leaned back, closed her eyes, and let out a long exhale. "Though, not going to lie, I could get used to this."

Jack leaned over and pulled out a bottle of champagne from a chilled drawer, quickly removed the foil, and sent the cork flying towards the back of the plane with a pop.

"Jesus," Sarah said, opening her eyes. "No sudden noises on the airplane, please?"

Jack smiled and tipped back the bottle.

Sarah cocked her head sideways and stared curiously at Jack. "Are there no glasses onboard?"

Jack laughed, brought the bottle up to his lips, and took another sip. "Who needs glasses? Just more to clean up, right?"

Sarah held her hand out for the bottle, but Jack pulled it like a teddy bear to his chest. "I'm not a fan of sharing," he said.

Sarah laughed and yanked the bottle out of his hands. "I think CJ would disagree."

A slow rumble began as the flight crew started up one engine, followed shortly by the other. As the aircraft started to taxi, Jack smiled and raised his eyebrows.

Sarah handed the champagne bottle back to Jack and unbuckled her seat belt.

"Babe, you need to keep that on until we are in the air."

She smiled and stood up just long enough to remove her panties.

"Oh," Jack said with a grin. "I guess that'll be okay."

Pulling her skirt up a little and spreading her legs, Sarah reached her hand down and firmly cupped herself. Without breaking eye contact with Jack, Sarah used two fingers to slowly rub circles around her clit. Jack leaned back, took another sip of champagne, and carefully repositioned the growing erection in his pants.

Sarah unbuttoned the top of her blouse and unfastened her bra. She carefully exposed enough of her breasts so that Jack could see her erect nipples. Rubbing her clit, pinching a nipple, Sarah leaned back and closed her eyes.

"You better slow down," Jack said with a soft laugh. "You'll be finished long before we hit the mile mark."

"It's a five-hour flight. Pretty sure you'll give me another chance," she said.

"Does that mean you aren't waiting on me?"

Sarah lifted her head and opened her eyes without stopping her self-stimulation. "Who said you weren't invited this time?" she asked through a bit of a grin. With that, she leaned her head back, closed her eyes, and continued to rub.

Jack looked out the window, then towards the cockpit, and finally back at his wife. The plane wasn't even out to the runway.

"But if you're going to join me, you better hurry."

Jack was the ultimate rule follower. He never painted outside the lines. But this? *Fuck the FAA*.

He quickly unbuckled his seatbelt, unzipped his pants, released his erection, and fell to his knees in front of his wife. Sarah reached down, grabbed his cock, and gently guided him inside her. Smiling, she began to speak in sentences broken up by Jack's thrusting. "Ladies and gentlemen...welcome onboard Flight 69... with service from...New Jersey to Seattle."

Jack couldn't help but laugh as he tried to find a better angle to enter his wife. The chair was too tall for him to reach her properly on his knees.

Sarah pulled her skirt higher as she slid lower in the chair. Wrapping her arms and legs around him, she continued. "We are currently...third in line for take-off...and are expected to be...in the air in... approximately two minutes."

Jack, still not happy with their position, pulled away from Sarah to grab a pillow from a nearby chair for him to kneel on.

"We ask that you please fasten your seatbelts at this time and secure all baggage underneath your seat or in the overhead compartments," Sarah said with a smile as he got his pillow squared away. She unfastened the buttons on his shirt and continued with her preflight briefing. "We also ask that... your seat, tray table...and penis all remain...in the upright position...for take-off."

"You've lost it," Jack said, approaching orgasm.

"Please turn off...all personal...electronic devices... including laptops...and cell phones...Smoking is prohibited... for the duration of the flight... except for our newest members...of the Mile High Club."

"Fuck, I'm close."

Sarah laughed and pulled Jack back into her grasp of arms and legs. "I think you were a little distracted. I already came."

As the jet accelerated down the runway, Jack came in his wife. Holding her in his arms, he laughed as he tried to catch his breath.

With her mouth by his ear, she whispered, "On behalf of the captain and crew, I thank you for flying Mile High Airlines."

CHAPTER NINETEEN

The hotel was only a fifteen-minute ride from the airport. Sarah had hoped to see more of the city before dinner, but it was too late by the time they got situated in their room.

"I would order a bottle of champagne from room service," Jack said to Sarah while she was showering. "But I'm concerned that the odds are pretty good that tonight will be a heavy vodka drinking night."

"I thought that was just in the movies," Sarah replied.

"I think it's a thing—either way, better to be safe than sorry."

When Jack and Sarah stepped outside the hotel's front entrance, Viktor Kozlov's limo driver stood beside the car waiting on them. Sarah had joked with Jack earlier that she felt like they were in a James Bond movie and about to be whisked away to an evil villain's secret lair. Jack assured her that the wheat magnate they were joining for dinner was no evil villain, but Sarah wasn't so sure based on the look of his driver.

Her visions of billionaire mansions with beautiful grounds

came crashing down as the limo came to a stop. Sarah didn't want to get out of the car, much less enter one of these buildings to eat a meal. Half the nearby buildings had broken windows, the neighborhood was rundown and dirty, and she was convinced that the only smell outside the vehicle would be garbage and urine. Looking down the narrow steps to the darkly lit restaurant entrance, all Sarah could think of was that it was the perfect place to get mugged.

The limo driver briskly walked around and opened the door.

"What kind of billionaire would eat at a place like this?" she asked, making no move to get out of the car.

"The kind who wants to eat the best solyanka in America," the limo driver said with a heavy Russian accent yet no facial expression.

Jack turned to Sarah, looking for permission to get out of the car. She gave him a nasty look and shooed him out of the door. "If we're going, let's go."

Stepping out onto the sidewalk, Sarah was pleasantly surprised by an odor emanating from the restaurant's entrance.

"It's the solyanka," the driver said when he caught Sarah sniffing the air. "If we were in Moscow, all you would smell is gasoline and construction."

Jack led the way down the stairs and slowly pulled the heavy wooden door open to reveal a lively, beautiful interior. The entranceway was small, but it opened to a bar on the left and a large room with only a dozen or so tables on the right. Decorated with dark wood and red velvet wall coverings with ornate chandeliers hanging from the ceiling, the restaurant looked like a scene from a movie. The contrast between the dreary outside and the beautiful, clean inside was remarkable, though smoke filled the air making it clear that a nonsmoking section was out of the question.

The maître d' looked up as Jack approached. "Mr. Williams?" he asked before Jack could say a word.

"Yes," Jack said, taken by surprise. "We are here to see...."

"Mr. Kozlov," the maître d' interrupted. "Follow me."

Jack and Sarah shared a quick look before falling in step behind the man.

They followed him through the main room into a back hallway that opened up into a small, private dining room. Two large men standing to either side of the entrance looked them up and down as they approached, likely making a quick assessment that they posed no threat to their boss. Pausing just outside the door, the maître d' announced into the room, "Mr. Jack Williams and guest."

"Come in, come in," came a loud voice with an equally thick Russian accent. The two men parted just enough that Jack and Sarah could only squeeze through one at a time. Jack stepped through first, holding Sarah's hand securely as she followed.

"Mr. Jack Williams?" the man standing by the table asked.

"Yes, and my wife, Sarah."

"Hello, Mr. Jack Williams and Sarah. I am Viktor Dmitrievich Kozlov," he said, holding his hand to his chest. "This is Polina," he said, gesturing to a strikingly beautiful woman with black hair and a curvaceous body seated by his side who couldn't be more than twenty-one or twenty-two years old.

"Very nice to meet you both," Jack said.

"Sit, please, sit," Viktor commanded.

Sarah looked over at Polina, who was the personification of a Russian Barbie doll, if such a thing existed. "My God, Viktor," Sarah said, cutting her sentence short. "I'm sorry. May I call you Viktor?"

"Yes, please. If I may call you Sarah."

"Of course," she said.

"Continue," Viktor encouraged her. "What were you going to say?"

"I was going to say how stunning Polina is. Your wife is beautiful."

Viktor smiled, but the look on Polina's face remained expressionless. "Sarah, my wife is beautiful, but Polina is not my wife."

Sarah held her hand up over her mouth. "Mr. Kozlov, Polina, please forgive me."

Viktor smiled a reassuring smile and slightly bowed his head. "Viktor, please. And it is fine." He turned to face Jack. "Now, Mr. Jack Williams, in Russia, it is custom to begin a new business relationship with a drink." Looking over at the server standing against the wall, Viktor waved him over to the table. "Vodka. Seychas."

The server walked over to a bucket of ice on a table against the wall and pulled out a bottle of vodka, immediately handing it to Kozlov.

Turning to the table, Viktor poured four shots of vodka. "To our new business relationship," he said. He set the bottle of vodka down and raised his glass. "And to our new friendship." He held his glass high in the center of the table.

Sarah looked at Jack, who simply nodded and met Viktor's glass over the table. The two women followed in kind.

"Vashe zdorov'ye!" Viktor said.

Sarah paused before drinking and looked at him.

"To your health," Viktor said.

Sarah nodded and then downed the vodka in one quick motion.

"Sarah," Viktor said, laughing. "Maybe you have a little Russian in you, no?"

"Maybe," she said, wiping vodka off her lips with the back of her hand.

Viktor lifted the bottle and quickly poured a second round.

Jack held his hand up in the universal stop motion. "Viktor, we should probably eat a little something first," Jack said.

"Yes, Mr. Jack Williams, if you want to insult me, we can eat first."

Jack looked briefly at Sarah before he reached out and lifted his glass. "Vashe zdorov'ye," Jack said with his best effort. The others brought their glasses up to meet in the middle and drank the vodka.

"Good choice," Viktor said. "Now, the food."

"Is there a menu?" Sarah asked.

"No menus," Viktor said.

"No menus?" Sarah replied.

"Not when you dine with me," he said.

Four excellent courses, and even more rounds of vodka, later, Sarah gave Jack one of her I'm-about-to-say-something-you-aren't-going-to-like looks. Jack immediately glared at her and shook his head slightly.

Viktor noticed the exchange out of the corner of his eye. "What is this you say to your wife with no words?"

Jack leaned back in his chair and let out a long exhale while he tried to decide his best course of action.

"We are friends, no?" Viktor asked. "What is it that you don't want her to say to new friends?"

"Viktor, we have a saying in this country," Jack said. "Curiosity killed the cat."

"Lyubopytnoy Varvare na bazare nos otorvali," Viktor said. "But in our version, it is a Barbara and not a cat."

"And Barbara does not die," Polina added. "She loses nose."

Jack smiled at both of them. "Well, I don't want Sarah to die or lose a nose, so...."

Viktor laughed. "I promise, Jack, no matter what Sarah asks, she will leave tonight with both her life and her nose."

Sarah smiled at Viktor. "That's a promise?"

"On my life," he answered with a slight bow.

"Okay, here goes," she said, looking at Jack out of the corner of her eye. "Why don't you bring your wife with you when you travel?" Sarah asked with a prevalent slur. "Why do you leave her at home?"

The smile quickly disappeared from Viktor's face. "I'm not used to speaking so directly with stranger," Viktor said, looking over at Jack. "In fact, I don't speak of such things with anyone."

"Viktor, I apologize for my wife. It was a question like this that I was worried about, especially because we are new friends," Jack said, adding one more thing to his list of regrets for the evening. Bringing Sarah. Allowing Viktor to pour round after round of vodka. Not immediately changing the subject when Sarah started asking questions about Viktor's wife in front of Viktor's mistress. Jack needed to bring the evening to a close before Sarah permanently damaged the relationship. How could he return to New York and tell Greg that he lost a fifty-million-dollar account because Sarah got drunk and interrogated their client about his marriage?

"Don't apologize for me, Jack," Sarah said, annoyed that he was treating her like a child. "I'm a big girl."

"We have saying in Russia," Viktor said. "A spoken word is not a sparrow. Once it flies out, you can't catch it."

Sarah continued as if she didn't hear a word he said. "Listen, all I'm saying is that I don't understand why you would bring a mistress with you rather than your wife."

"My wife stays home with children," Viktor said.

"Can't someone else stay home with children? Don't you think your wife would enjoy coming to Seattle with you?" She looked up at his companion. "No offense, Polina, you seem like a lovely girl."

"This is not my wife's life," Viktor replied. "She makes home for me. For my children."

"Do you love her?"

"Do I love my wife?"

"Yes."

"I worship the ground she walks on. I can't live without her love."

"Yet you bring Polina?"

"Mrs. Williams..." Viktor protested.

"Please call me Sarah," she insisted.

Viktor looked up at Jack. "I am sorry, Mr. Jack Williams, but may I speak with your wife about such things that men and women do not normally speak?"

Jack let out a long exhale. "Viktor, you are welcome to discuss anything you would like with my wife. Or, we can move on with a dessert course."

Viktor turned to Polina. "Ty ne vozrazhayete, yesli ya rasskazhu o nashey seksual'noy zhizni?"

Without expression, Polina replied, "Eto luchshe, chem kogda ty govorish' o svoyey zhene."

"Sarah, there are things I do with Polina that I would never do with the mother of my children," Viktor said.

"Why?" Sarah asked.

"Because I enjoy them," he replied.

"No, I mean, why don't you do them with your wife?"

"Because she is the mother of my children."

"Let me ask you this, Viktor, do you think your wife might enjoy them if you would give her a chance?"

"These things? No," Viktor said with great confidence.

"Why not?" Sarah pried.

Viktor looked over at Jack in disbelief. "Because she is the mother of my children."

Sarah looked over at Polina. "These things that you do together do you enjoy them?"

"Yes, of course," Polina answered quietly. "Most of them," she clarified.

"So, Viktor, if Polina enjoys these things, why wouldn't your wife?"

Viktor was finally beginning to show signs of frustration. "Because she is the mother of my children," Viktor said slowly as if Sarah didn't speak English.

Sarah continued undeterred. "You say you love her. You say you worship the ground she walks on. Yet, you deny her these pleasures that you aren't willing to deny yourself." Sarah leaned back and finished the glass of vodka in front of her. "You are willing to give Polina these pleasures but not the woman you worship?"

Viktor raised his hand to get the waiter's attention. "Yeshche odnu butylku, pozhaluysta."

Jack quickly leaned in. "I don't know what you just said, Viktor, but if it involved more vodka, I'm not sure that's a great idea."

"It's ok, Mr. Jack Williams," Viktor said. He turned to Sarah and made eye contact. "Sarah, we have another saying in Russia. Don't go to another monastery with your own rules."

"I'm not sure what point you're trying to make," Sarah replied.

"I should not come to your country and question how you live. I did not know that Americans were so open about such things."

Jack quickly chimed in, "Viktor, I don't want you to leave this meal thinking Sarah is an average American. She is...different."

Viktor sat quietly for a second. "Different, yes. But different can be special, too, no?"

Jack smiled. "Yes, she is that as well," Jack said, extending his drink across the table to toast with Viktor. "I just hope that her being special hasn't offended you."

"No, I find what she says…interesting." Viktor turned to Sarah. "Sarah, tell me the truth, you think I should go home and do these bad things to my wife?"

"No, Viktor," Sarah replied. "I think you should go home and do these bad things *with* your wife."

Viktor seemed to ponder what Sarah had said as he poured another round of drinks.

"YA khochu byt' tam, kogda ty zasunesh' svoy bol'shoy chlen v yeye malen'kuyu devstvennuyu popku," Polina said under her breath.

"Polina!" Viktor snapped.

"What? It's true," she replied in English.

Viktor leaned across the table and met Jack's glass with his own. "This is not the evening I expected, Mr. Jack Williams."

"It was different, eh?" Jack asked.

"Different and special," Viktor said, nodding to Sarah. "Za zdorov'ye."

"Za zdorov'ye," the others replied in unison.

CHAPTER TWENTY

Walking through the hotel lobby, Sarah noticed their pilot at the bar. "Jack, look, it's Maddie. Come on. I want to talk with her," she said, grabbing Jack's arm as she pulled him in that direction.

Jack was concerned that Sarah's level of curiosity, mixed with almost two bottles of vodka shared between the four of them, was cause for concern. "Sarah, don't bother the woman."

"She's sitting alone at a bar. I'm sure she wouldn't mind some company."

Maddie saw Sarah approaching out of the corner of her eye and turned to face them. "Well, don't you two look like the happy couple?"

"Hello, Maddie, how are you?" Sarah asked, plopping herself down in a seat at the bar and taking Maddie's hand in her own.

"I'm good, thanks."

Jack frowned at Sarah. Turning to Maddie, he said, "It may be a little late to ask, but do you mind if we join you?"

Maddie smile. "Technically, I'm not supposed to fraternize

with my passengers, but I was here first, so...happy to have the company."

Sarah continued to rub Maddie's arm. "Seeing you sitting here by yourself made me realize that we may have taken you away from your husband or kids."

"Divorced. No kids, so it's all good," she replied.

Jack smiled and dropped one of his favorite lines. "For the record, we always thought he was a jerk."

Maddie smiled and took a sip of her bourbon. "Well, first of all, he is a she... and secondly, you would probably love her."

"I am so sorry," Jack said quickly.

Maddie looked at Jack and smiled. "Are you sorry that I'm a lesbian or sorry my marriage didn't work out?"

"Neither. Both," Jack choked, trying to get the words out. "I don't know what I'm saying," he stammered. "I'm just going to stop talking and order a drink."

Maddie laughed and turned to Sarah. "Is he always this easy to screw with?"

"Yes. Always," Sarah said with a smile.

The ladies continued to talk as Jack tried to get the bartender's attention.

"Since my husband has already embarrassed us, do you mind if I ask what happened in your marriage? It seems odd to hear someone speak so highly of an ex."

"I don't mind. Long story short. Her name is Becky. We dated in college and survived some pretty big obstacles over the years. We came out to our families together. Got married right before I went into the Air Force. We managed to overcome all the trials and tribulations of deployments and discrimination and acceptance issues from others, and then...."

"And then?" Sarah asked.

"And then I got out of the Air Force, and everything was perfect."

Sarah let out a small laugh. "And then?"

"And then Becky decided she wanted children," Maddie said, taking a sip.

"Oh no," Sarah said. "And that wasn't in the cards for you?"

"Ironically, it's something we never discussed. I wanted to travel the world, which is why I took this job. Execs from the firm fly to some beautiful places, and what do you know...it's much cheaper to put me up in a hotel to wait for them than it is for me to fly back to pick them up later."

"And kids were a deal-breaker for Becky?"

"Kids were a deal-breaker for both of us," she said. "It was a painful decision, but the right one. Someone who wants to raise a kid should walk through fire to do it. And someone who doesn't want to raise a child? Well, if they can help it, they never should."

When there was a break in the conversation, Jack handed a champagne glass to Sarah but hesitated before giving one to Maddie. "I'm not sure what the rules are. I see you already have a drink. Are you allowed to have another?"

Maddie smiled. "I'm good as long as you two don't plan on flying anywhere in the next eight hours."

Jack smiled and handed her the champagne glass. "I think you're safe."

Looking at the drink, Maddie asked, "What is this?"

"It's a Kir Royale, crème de cassis topped with champagne," Jack said. He held his glass up to toast. "It's also a peace offering for that whole fiasco earlier."

Clinking glasses, Maddie said, "No apology necessary. Cheers."

Sarah took a sip and placed her glass on the bar. Turning

to Maddie, she continued. "So, you two just split up, stopped on a dime?"

"It wasn't that quick. We discussed it over six months or so, at which point we both came to the same conclusion."

"I'm so sorry. It's so sad."

Staring into space across the bar, Maddie said, "It was sad. We cried a lot. We laughed a lot. In some ways, it felt like someone was dying."

"Do you ever see her?"

"I better. I'm the godmother to her daughter."

"Are you kidding me?" Sarah asked.

"Nope."

"I don't even know how to process that," Sarah said.

Sarah, Jack, and Maddie sat there for another hour or so, talking about everything: Maddie's goddaughter, Colin, flying, travel, life goals, the best cities, the rudest cities. Sarah and Jack had a couple more drinks, though Maddie moved on to decaf. About the time that Jack was going to suggest that it was time for bed, Sarah got the same look on her face she had at dinner with Viktor.

"Please don't?" Jack asked with little confidence in preventing her.

Sarah just gave him a silly look and continued. "Maddie, can I ask you something completely inappropriate?"

Jack immediately cut in. "Okay, that's enough. I think it's time for bed."

Maddie just laughed. "Sure, go right ahead."

Sarah did a nervous double-take between Jack and Maddie. Jack finally just shrugged his shoulders.

"Do you know what we were doing in the back of the plane during the flight?" Sarah asked with a face scrunched up like Maddie might punch her.

Maddie just laughed. "Of course."

"And you don't mind?"

"Mind? Seattle's a long flight. We appreciate the entertainment. Chad and I normally take bets."

"Wait a minute. You can hear everything?"

"Well, we can't hear everything, but there isn't much of a divider between the cockpit and the cabin. So, if people are loud, or... possibly engaging in sex before the engines are completely spun up, like, say, while we are taxiing...."

Jack poked Sarah's arm. "That's on you!"

Sarah turned beet red. "Oh my god, I want to die."

Maddie reached out and took Sarah's hand. "Don't feel bad. You won me twenty bucks."

"Are you kidding? You bet Chad that we would have sex before we took off?"

"No, we bet the over-under."

Sarah looked to Jack to see if he understood what she meant, but it was clear that he didn't have a clue either. Looking back to Maddie, she asked, "Okay, what's that mean?"

"The bet is whether or not you will wait until we reach cruising altitude. Technically it only takes five thousand two hundred and eighty feet to qualify for the mile-high club, but we hit that pretty fast."

Sarah laughed as she rubbed Maddie's hand. "I guess we didn't quite make it."

"Not even close," Maddie said with a smile. "It's a new company record as far as I know."

Jack leaned in and smiled. "Okay, full disclosure, why did you bet the under?"

Maddie looked back and forth between the two of them. "Younger couple relative to most of the others. Shorter skirt than most of the others. And not only did it appear that you two loved each other, but it also seemed like you actually liked each other."

Sarah looked up at Jack and smiled. "All true."

Jack pulled his chair closer as if he was about to share a secret. "Okay, since we're all in, let me ask you this. How many different execs have joined the Mile High Club with the company jet?"

Maddie took a sip of her coffee before answering. "Giving out information like that might get me fired."

"Come on, give me a ballpark?" Jack asked.

Maddie thought for a second before answering. "I'm honestly not comfortable sharing that information, as I would never share it about you two. However, I will say this, if you were to look at the flight manifest, for any flight with more than one person and no flight attendant...it's a pretty safe bet."

Jack replayed what she said in his mind. "Wait, more than one? Are you saying what I think you're saying?"

"I'm not saying anything," Maddie said with a grin.

"Hang on, so you are talking about more than two or more than three or...." He paused. "More than four?"

"I'm saying, any number more than one...without a flight attendant." Maddie took her last sip of coffee and stood up from her chair. "Unless it's McGivens. He just doesn't like people."

Jack looked over at Sarah. "She's not wrong."

Maddie offered her hand to Jack. "Thank you for the drinks. I enjoyed getting to know you both."

"Our pleasure," Jack said, shaking her hand.

Maddie turned and smiled at Sarah. "Now, my turn. If you will allow me a brief moment to be inappropriate."

Sarah laughed. "Of course. That's the least I can do."

Maddie leaned in, kissed Sarah on the cheek, and hugged her. "You are adorable. If I were just a little younger...and you weren't married...and, you know, you were gay...I might have very much enjoyed not raising children with you."

Sarah blushed as she slowly withdrew from Maddie's

embrace. Sarah did a double-take between Maddie and Jack. The comment was so forward yet felt genuine. Sarah had no idea what to say. When she mumbled a few words that never completely left her lips, Maddie leaned in and kissed her cheek one more time. "Exactly," she said. "Good night."

Jack and Sarah sat in silence as they watched her walk toward the hotel elevators. Finally, Jack broke the silence. "Do you want to skip a few?"

"I don't understand," Sarah replied.

"Fantasy seven. Have sex with a woman."

Sarah didn't respond immediately.

"Do you want me to try to catch her?" Jack asked.

Sarah reached out and grabbed his hand. "No. Not tonight."

"You sure?"

"Yeah, I think I would like to make love with my husband."

Jack laughed and stood up. "You'll never hear me complain about that."

Sarah stood up and fell into step with Jack. "If it's okay with you, maybe I can bring Maddie back to bed with us tonight...in words."

Jack squeezed her hand and quickened his pace. "Yeah, I think that will work."

CHAPTER TWENTY-ONE

The flight home promised to be significantly less exciting than the flight out. After climbing the stairs to the jet, Sarah stuck her head into the cockpit to say hello to Maddie and Chad. "Listen, if you guys could avoid the potholes, that would be great."

"Hello, Sarah," Maddie replied. "A little too much fun last night?"

"Maybe a tad. But it was worth it," she said with a smile.

"Well, once you two get settled in, we will be on our way," Maddie said.

Jack was already situated by the time Sarah turned back towards the cabin. As she took her seat, he gave her a dirty look.

"What did I do wrong?" she asked.

"You didn't wear a skirt."

Sarah laughed and patted him on the leg. "Good lord, Jack, I think you'll be okay." Sitting down in her chair, she buckled her seatbelt and pulled out a book.

"Well, you're going to be great company," Jack said.

"What's that?"

"Look at you: no skirt, reading a book. You aren't going to be much fun on the trip back."

"Sorry, Jack, it looks like you're going to have to entertain yourself for the next few hours."

Jack leaned back in his seat and looked out the window as the jet took off. A few minutes into the flight, he could see a mountain off in the distance. He pointed out the window. "Hey babe, look. Pretty sure that's Mt. Rainier."

Sarah closed her book, carefully keeping her place with her finger, and looked out the window. "Pretty cool, Jack," she said with a smile. She immediately returned her attention to her book. "I mean, not quite as exciting as the flight out, but better than nothing, right?"

Jack fidgeted in his chair. "Why do you read stuff like that?" Jack asked about Sarah's ongoing relationship with romance novels.

"They make me happy."

"I thought I made you happy?"

"Well, I can enjoy both, can't I?" Without looking up, she added, "Besides, they always have a happy ending, something I think you would appreciate."

Jack continued to fidget.

"Jack, you are worse than Colin. Are you going to stare at me for the whole flight?" Sarah asked without looking up.

"Unless I find something better to do."

She closed her book. "Why don't you go up front and see if Maddie will let you fly the plane."

Jack perked up. "Do you think she would let me?"

"I was kidding, but by all means, go ask."

Jack hopped out of his seat and stuck his head into the cockpit. He had to laugh when he saw Maddie reading a romance novel as well.

"Everything okay, Mr. Williams?" Maddie asked over her shoulder.

"Yeah, just bored. Figured I would come to see if things were more exciting up here."

Maddie laughed. "The flight out always seems more exciting than the flight back." She closed her book and looked over her shoulder. "Did you want to take my seat for a bit?"

"Is that allowed?"

"Sure."

"If you don't mind, I would love it," Jack said. "Maybe you can do a better job entertaining Sarah than I can."

"I doubt that."

"Well, you're welcome to try."

Maddie turned more in her seat to face Jack better. "Do you mean that?"

"Sure, I'll keep Chad company for a while. The view up here is much better."

Maddie unbuckled her seat and placed her book into a side pocket. "I would disagree," she said with a smile as she climbed out of her seat.

Jack didn't dare ask Chad if he could take the controls, but he did ask a lot of questions. Jack considered going to the Naval Academy when he was in high school, but in the end, he decided he wasn't a fan of having people tell him what to do.

Chad politely answered all of his questions and shared a couple of stories about flying in the Navy. If Jack ever had doubts about skipping that life, the stories Chad told him put his mind at ease. A little over twenty minutes passed before Maddie appeared over his shoulder and quietly listened to them talk. Jack asked her if she was ready to switch back.

"If you've had enough," she said.

"I don't think I could ever get enough of this, but I'm certain Chad has had enough of me," he said, climbing out of the seat.

"No, we're good, Mr. Williams. You're welcome back anytime," Chad said.

Passing Maddie, Jack asked, "Everything good back there?"

"Everything was great, Jack," she said, gently grabbing his arm. "Thank you. You're a good man."

"No," Jack said, "thank you."

Walking into the cabin, Jack found Sarah sprawled backward in her seat drinking a beer.

"Well, don't you look relaxed."

Taking a sip of beer, Sarah looked up and smiled. "Holy shit, Jack, it's true what they say."

"Oh yeah? What do they say?" Jack said with a smile.

"The whole girl-on-girl thing."

Jack laughed as he took his seat. "That's what you ladies were talking about? She must be quite persuasive if she convinced you of that in less than twenty minutes."

"Oh, it didn't take twenty minutes," she said with a grin.

Jack looked at her and cocked his head sideways. "What are you saying?"

"I'm saying Maddie was amazing."

Jack scooted forward in his seat and stared at the ground between them. "Are you saying what I think you're saying?"

Sarah saw Jack's face and sat straight up in her chair. "Wait, what are you saying?"

Jack looked up and made eye contact. "I'm saying that it sounds like you let someone stimulate your vagina without my consent."

Sarah put her beer down and brought a hand over her mouth. "Jesus, Jack. It's not like that."

"Oh really. Then how do you see it?"

Sarah reached out and tried to take Jack's hand, but he pulled it away as she grabbed for it. "We discussed this. You sent her back here," she implored.

"No, Sarah, we didn't discuss *this,* and I certainly didn't send her back here to do *that*."

"Jack, are you kidding me?"

"Haven't we had this conversation before?" Jack asked sarcastically.

"You sent her out here to fulfill my girl-on-girl fantasy, right?"

"No, I sent her out here to keep you company."

"*Come back and entertain me*. That's what she said. I thought that's what you meant."

Jack pulled open the cooling drawer and grabbed a beer of his own. Sarah dropped to her knees and held his leg.

"I would never do something on purpose to hurt you in a million years," she whispered in a wounded voice.

"Please, just give me a minute," he said, staring forward into space, occasionally taking a sip of beer.

She reached her hand up his pant leg and began to rub his calf. "We talked about this, and you said you were okay with it."

"Sarah, we always discussed me being there with you," he said.

"She said entertain me. I never thought it meant anything else."

Jack took another sip of beer. "We should really work on our communication."

"Agreed. I'm so sorry."

"Are we really at a place where you will just have sex with anyone willing to entertain you?"

"Shit, you know it isn't like that. It was the perfect storm of circumstances and misunderstandings."

"I just really wanted to be there," he said again.

Sarah moved in front of him and began to unbuckle his belt.

"Especially your first time," he continued in a voice like a disappointed child.

When Sarah unzipped his pants, Jack's erection eagerly awaited her on the other side of his underwear. Taking him in her hand and navigating it through the fly, she added, "Does this mean you forgive me?" she asked, trying to control her smile as she began to stroke him.

"Sarah, you hurt my feelings. So, forgiven? Yes," he said as he scooted lower in the chair. "Forgotten? Not even close." He struggled to suppress a smile as he quoted Sarah's words back to her.

"I'll take what I can get," Sarah said before taking him into her mouth.

Jack closed his eyes and imagined the scene that he missed between Sarah and Maddie. It may not have been close to the real thing, but it didn't matter. In the end, it was the shortest blowjob Sarah had ever given.

CHAPTER TWENTY-TWO

Colin rushed down the sidewalk to greet them as the limo stopped in front of their house.

"Mommy!" Colin squealed.

Sarah quickly stepped out on the curb to hug him. "Hello, Colin. Were you good for Granna?"

"Yes. She bought me a book about trucks," he said with great joy.

"She did?"

"Yup! We went to the bookstore, and I got a book, and then we went for ice cream because I was so good."

Jack walked around the limo and lifted Colin in his arms. "Hey, buddy, I missed you."

"I missed you, too, Daddy."

Yuri carried their luggage up to the house and greeted Sarah's mother, who was standing just inside the door. "Good afternoon, Maureen."

"Hello, Yuri," she said as she stepped outside with her bags.

"Hi, Mom," Sarah said as she climbed the stairs to the

front porch. "Do you want to stay for dinner? Jack's going to run down to Panda Garden to grab some food."

"No. Thank you," Maureen said as she walked past Sarah without making eye contact. She paused briefly to kiss Colin as she passed Jack. After she put her bag into the trunk of her car, she looked up as she was about to climb in the driver's side door.

"Sarah, I left something for you in the kitchen. It would mean a lot to me if you would read it."

Sarah was terrified of what that could be, but she didn't feel that she had a choice given the situation. "Sure, Mom. I can do that."

"Thank you," she said as she climbed in and shut the door. Maureen glanced up briefly before gunning the accelerator.

"I love you, too," Sarah said to the back of the car as it drove away.

Jack walked up beside her. "Okay, I have growing concerns that you're no longer the favorite daughter."

Sarah took Colin from Jack. "I'm afraid you're right. I should let Ashley know. Though, I don't think she will be excited by the news."

Jack laughed. "That's true. Your sister has never cared much about what your mother thinks."

"My sister has never cared at all about what anyone thinks. Ever. But that's probably why I am the favorite. Or was. I care too much."

Yuri came out of the house and paused just outside the front door. "Will you be needing anything else?" he asked.

"No, Yuri. We're all set. Thanks for everything," Jack said, shaking his hand.

Sarah put Colin down just inside the front door and headed to the kitchen to find out what she had just committed to reading. Placed squarely in the center of the kitchen island was a hardback book with a shiny black cover with a blood-red font for the title and the author's name: *The Unmaking of a Lady* by Thomas L'Costa.

Jack walked into the kitchen to find Sarah with disbelief on her face. "What's wrong?" Jack asked.

"My mother left me a gift," she said, holding up the book for Jack to read the cover.

"The unmaking of a lady? That sounds ominous. Is there any chance I'm not the bad guy in this, my lady?"

"I would guess zero," Sarah said as she opened up the book cover to read the inside flap. "When she first met Mr. Wonderful, everyone loved him. He was intelligent, funny, good-looking, and extremely charismatic. It may have taken a few weeks, a few months, or in some cases, over a year, but eventually, everyone began to see the cracks except for her. Whether she is your daughter or sister or your divorced or widowed mother, she slowly becomes distant and withdrawn. She swears everything is fine. They are madly in love, she says. But she doesn't keep the same friends as before if any. You see her less and less. And one day, probably when you least expect it, you get a peek behind the curtain and realize that she is under his control, an object of his desires. Yet, she still swears it's love."

Sarah looked up from the book. "Ok, I'm concerned that you aren't the favorite son-in-law."

"I'm her only son-in-law."

"I know. That's the part that concerns me."

"If she only knew...."

"She doesn't need to know, Jack."

Lifting the book back up, Sarah continued. "Pulling from his deep experience with treating recovering victims of cult leaders...." Sarah looked up at Jack. "Oh lord," she said before continuing. "Author Thomas L'Costa shows us a world not seen by many people. *The Unmaking of a Lady* is a remarkable journey into the depths of human manipulation, degradation, and the sexual exploitation of women from all walks of life. L'Costa will demonstrate that nobody is safe from the charisma of a cult-like personality. But there is hope. Thomas L'Costa provides detailed steps on removing your loved one from the sphere of such influence and shows you how to begin the journey back to recovery."

Sarah laid the book down and started to cry. Jack walked around the island and hugged her. "Jack," she said. "My mother thinks you turned me into a whore."

Jack held her as she cried. "I think we need to set your mother straight. It's not right for her to think I turned you into a whore," he said, squeezing her tight. "We both know it's Monica's fault."

"Shut up, Jack," she said as a little laugh escaped. "That's not funny."

"You know I'm just teasing you. If you want my honest opinion? You are living out your fantasies with the man you love. How is that a bad thing?"

"It's not that easy."

"Sure it is. I love you. You love me. And anything that we are doing is with consenting adults. Why do you care what others think?"

Sarah squeezed him back before pulling free from his embrace. "How would you like to discuss this with your mother?" she asked as she grabbed a beer out of the fridge. "Want one?"

"Please."

"So, would you like to discuss this with your mother or not?"

"Sarah, you know I don't want to discuss this with my mom. I don't want to discuss anything of a sexual nature with her."

"But what if she found out and bought you books about treating your perversion?"

Jack took a sip of his beer. "I would simply tell her it's none of her business, and that would be the end of it."

"That's not fair. Your family doesn't talk about anything anyway."

"True, and we certainly won't be breaking with that tradition on this one."

"Well, then you can't begin to relate."

Jack sat down on a stool at the kitchen island. "Are you saying you want to stop? No more fantasies? No more club?" He paused. "No more CJ?"

"Sitting here in our kitchen, holding the book my mother bought to save me from a life of sexual submission, to save me from you...I don't know how we can keep doing it."

Jack got up from his stool and walked in front of the bay window facing their backyard. The leaves were beginning to turn oranges and reds, some already free and blowing across the yard. It was quite peaceful. He wondered why everything in life couldn't be this calm.

"Jack?" Sarah said, bringing his thoughts back to the room.

"Do you regret any of the things we've done?" Jack asked.

Sarah got up from her stool and sat down on the loveseat in front of him. "No. I don't regret any of it."

"And other than it feeling wrong, do you think we actually did anything wrong?"

"No, Jack. I don't."

"And be honest, do you feel that I have pushed you into this? Because to tell you the truth, I didn't give you much choice. Maybe I am the manipulative charismatic cult leader after all."

Sarah grabbed Jack's hand and pulled him close, burying her head against his stomach. "All you did was open the door a crack, Jack, and I bolted through it like I was on fire."

Jack kissed the top of her head. "I think we have three

options: first, we stop completely, and you go back to living with adequate for the rest of your life."

Sarah pulled her head away from his chest and looked up. "That's not an option."

"Okay, then two, we continue down the path we were on and simply refuse to discuss it with your mother."

"And three?" she said with a hopeful voice.

"You sit your mother down and explain that you brought us here, that you enjoy this lifestyle, and you don't plan on changing."

"Good lord. There has to be another option."

"Okay, fine. We live with adequate until your mother dies, and then, assuming we aren't too old to have a sex life that's more than adequate, we get back to it."

"Nice, Jack. I'm sure I would really enjoy myself at the club after the funeral."

"Hey, you wanted another option."

Sarah walked to the island and grabbed the book. "Do you mind bringing Colin with you when you run to grab dinner? I'm going to climb into a hot bath and begin my deprogramming. If I become a lady again, maybe I'll be able to think more clearly."

Jack smiled. "That's fine and all, but when that warm water begins to run down your foot and over your leg, and your thoughts drift to the time you spent with Maddie, don't blame me when you find yourself propped up in that tub, letting the warm water run down over your clit. Because that's on you," he said with a fake, serious look.

"Seriously? Why would you do that? How do you expect me to focus on the book now?"

"I don't," he said with a smile.

"Thanks a lot," she said, walking out of the kitchen.

"The master manipulator strikes again!" he yelled after her.

CHAPTER TWENTY-THREE

"Can I see it?" Monica asked.

"No," Sarah replied.

"Sarah, I need to see it. You know how I am. You can't leave 'lifelike' to my imagination."

"I don't care. Let your imagination run wild."

"Well, then, can I have Marcus's phone number?"

"Monica, stop. It's not like he's a dress I can let you borrow," she said even as the thought of Marcus made her smile. "You're making me regret sharing any of this with you." Sarah had just given Monica details about their night with Marcus, but she didn't dare share anything about the list or the sex club.

Monica climbed down off the stool in the kitchen and grabbed a bottle of wine from the fridge.

"Hey, no alcohol," Sarah said, scolding her. "I asked you here to keep Colin for the night. If anything were to happen to him after you have been drinking, Jack would kill you," she said as she took the bottle of white wine and put it back in the fridge. "That is if I didn't kill you first."

"So just because your mom sees your slut clothes and an enormous black dick, I have to go to rehab for the evening?"

"Twenty-four hours, Monica. Do you think you can handle it?"

Monica sat back down on the stool while Sarah prepared food for the meals she would miss.

"I'm going to need one or the other," Monica said. "I'm going to need the lifelike or the Marcus guy's phone number."

Sarah glared over at Monica. "Jack should be home any minute. Please handle the details of my sex life a little more carefully."

Monica laid her arms and head down on the island in the kitchen and closed her eyes. "It's not fair, you know," Monica said.

"What's not fair?" Sarah asked, not looking up from her meal prep.

"You have a husband, yet somehow you get even more men."

"I'm a lucky girl."

"Yeah, but I don't have anyone. And you would rather ship me off to Alaska than share one of your extras."

Sarah looked over at Monica sprawled over the counter.

"Monica, if I had his number, I would give it to you."

"Do you mean that?"

"I do."

Monica sat up straight on her stool. "Thanks. That means a lot."

"Well, I'm happy to help."

"Now about that vibrator?"

It never crossed Sarah's mind that she and Jack would be going into the city for their regular monthly date night. With all the drama and uncertainty with her mother, she thought for sure Jack would let their standard monthly outing come and go without acknowledging it. Maureen was pressing Sarah to get some counseling from the one-and-only Thomas L'Costa, who conveniently lived in nearby Rye, New York, though inconveniently didn't hold a degree in counseling. Jack had different plans. He felt it was more important than ever to live their lives as they wanted.

Sitting in the back of the limo, opening the customary bottle of champagne, Jack expressed his thoughts on the situation. "It feels weird not being her favorite after all these years. I think your mother would literally like anyone else your sister brought home more than me."

"Clearly, you haven't met many of the men my sister has brought home."

"Honestly, the only thing worse than her refusing to look at me is when she makes eye contact," he said, making a shivering sound. "Brrr."

Sarah sat back in her seat and drank champagne. Looking out the window, she contemplated the activities in their life. "Do you think we're being selfish?" she asked.

"How so?"

"Going into the city. Going to sex clubs. Leaving Colin alone once a month just so that you can fulfill my sexual fantasies. Our behavior. All of it."

Jack took Sarah's hand and squeezed it. "Absolutely not."

"You sure about that?" she asked.

"Sarah, do you think it's a horrible thing for Colin to spend time with his grandmother?"

"Of course not."

"Most people would consider him lucky to have this experience in his life. Staying up past his bedtime. Eating food he shouldn't eat. Hearing stories about the grandfather he never met."

Sarah squeezed Jack's hand and looked out the window. They rode along for a few minutes in silence, watching the world slowly shift from the beautiful green trees of Connecticut to the towering gray buildings of Manhattan.

"Can you please tell me what fantasies are left on the list?" Sarah asked for the hundredth time.

"No."

"Will you at least tell me what fantasy you are trying to fulfill tonight?" she asked.

"I can neither confirm nor deny that we are even trying to tackle a fantasy tonight," he said, rubbing her leg. "How do you know tonight isn't all about me?" he asked.

"Sorry, mister, I am unaware of any fantasies you have to fulfill," she said, patting him on the leg.

Jack leaned in and kissed her. "I only have one fantasy," he said.

"And what is that?" she asked, kissing him back.

"Fulfilling yours."

Sarah smiled and looked back out of the window. "Well, you're doing a pretty good job so far."

"I know," he said.

Climbing out of the limo, Jack handed the bellman some money and asked him to take their bags to their room. Sarah looked at him quizzically. "And why aren't we going to the room?"

Jack turned to face her with a mischievous grin. "Meeting a friend at the bar for a quick drink."

"And so it begins," Sarah replied with a smile.

"Relax," Jack said. "It's not what you think."

Holding Jack's hand and following him into the bar, Sarah saw CJ speaking with an Asian gentleman on the far side of the room. He glanced up and smiled when he saw them. Taking a seat at the bar, Jack ordered a couple of vodka and sodas.

"One with lemon and one plain," a voice said to the bartender from over their shoulders. "And put them on the house, please."

"Of course, Mr. Johnson," the bartender replied, turning quickly to make the drinks.

Sarah stood and hugged CJ. Quickly backing away from the embrace, she blushed. "Sorry about that. I guess you probably don't hug many of your guests."

CJ just smiled. "I would prefer a more intimate greeting, but...probably best not to go down that road."

"No offense taken," she said.

Turning to Jack, he shook his hand and said, "I made sure that your favorite room is ready."

"Wait," Sarah chimed in. "Ready for what? Do you have a role to play in our evening? Because I can't get anything out of Jack."

CJ laughed as he pulled up a stool next to them and sat down. "Sorry, Sarah. You've already checked that box. My role tonight will be limited to that of the general manager of the Aspect East Village Hotel."

"Well, I'm not going to lie," Sarah said, turning to Jack. "That makes me a little sad," she said with a sly little grin.

"Full disclosure," CJ continued. "I'm aware of the details for tonight. You'll be in good hands."

Sarah turned back to the bar and lifted her drink. "In that case, I'm trusting you boys."

"Dammit," Jack said out of the blue.

"What's the matter?" Sarah replied.

"I left my wallet in my overnight bag, and CJ wanted to show us a new Sushi place before we go to the club. Do you mind running to the room and grabbing it for me while we wrap up a few details about the evening's plans?"

"Not at all, you little coconspirators," she said. "You boys plot away."

Grabbing a room key from the front desk, Sarah turned and walked across the lobby. She smiled as she caught the two of them staring at her with silly grins as she walked to the elevators. As she selected her floor and the doors began to close, a beautiful specimen of a man rushed on with her, barely sneaking in before the doors closed on him. Sarah smiled. "Not sure it was worth getting crushed," she said.

"Oh, I think it will be," he said as he grabbed her by the waist and tried to kiss her.

Sarah pushed him away and slapped him as hard as she could. "What the hell do you think you're doing?"

The man recoiled and retreated to the other side of the elevator. At about that exact moment, the elevator jerked to a stop.

"Damn, lady, he didn't say anything about pain."

"What did you say?" Sarah said while balling up her fists and assuming a fighting stance.

"We only have four minutes," the young man said. "Is this really how you want to spend them?"

Sarah blinked and tried to make sense of what he was saying. "What the hell are you talking about?"

"Your husband said that we only had four minutes before the elevator starts moving again," he said while rubbing his face.

"My husband told you to come in here and grab me?"

"No, he told me to come in here and fuck you."

Sarah looked down at the ground and lowered her fists. "Did he tell you that you should say something before you started trying to fuck me?"

"Dammit... yes," he said while literally scratching his head.

"And?"

"I can't remember."

"We're on the clock here...."

"Gerabaldo... Geronello..."

"Geronimo?"

"Yes, Geronimo!" the young man said, looking up with an excited face.

"Good lord," Sarah said as she grabbed him by the shoulders and pressed him to his knees. Lifting her skirt, she pulled her underwear to the side and guided his face between her legs.

The young man eagerly provided the service that was being requested.

"Gentle," Sarah said.

"I'm sorry," came a muffled reply.

"That's okay. Keep going."

After a moment, the young man began to moan while he provided the stimulation. It sounded more like he was enjoying a great meal than enjoying oral sex to Sarah. After an understandably rough start, he fell into a rhythm that worked for Sarah.

"There... that's it... just like that," she said.

The young man's moaning elevated to a new level. "Oh my god, this is so hot," he said. "You taste so good."

Sarah closed her eyes and focused on her favorite memory from her sexual highlight reel.

"Seriously, this is amazing," the young man continued.

Sarah rolled her eyes, though nobody could see her. "Hey," she said. "What's your name?"

"Tim," he said between moans.

"Tim, it's nice to meet you. Now please stop talking. I'm trying to focus."

"I'm sorry, I'm sorry," he said. A moment later, Tim began to moan again.

Sarah slapped him on the side of the head. "No moaning, either."

"I'm sorry. I'm sorry," he repeated.

After about a minute, Sarah asked, "Do you have a condom?"

"Yes. In my pocket."

"Okay, how quick can you get it on?"

"Probably quicker if you help," he said. "Seriously."

"Okay, that's fine. Just get it ready."

Without diverting his mouth's attention, Tim removed the condom from his pocket and held it up in the air for Sarah. She tore the packaging open and removed the condom.

"Okay, you ready?" she asked.

"Mmm-hmmm," came the reply.

"Go," Sarah urged as she dropped to her knees. Freeing his erection from his pants, Sarah quickly deep-throated him a couple of times before she placed the condom on. "You need to be quick," she said as she stood and faced the side of the elevator.

"I've been thinking about this for a week," Tim said. "Quick will not be my challenge."

Pulling her underwear down to her knees, she lifted her skirt and pushed her backside against him.

Tim was careful to enter her gently and slowly began to thrust.

"Tim, I appreciate you being gentle and all," Sarah said after a few seconds. "But that's not going to get me there with the time remaining. I'm going to need you to fuck me."

"Seriously?" he gasped.

"Seriously."

With that information, Tim placed one hand on her

shoulder and the other hand on her hip and began to pull her back into each thrust as hard as he could.

"There you go," Sarah offered as encouragement.

Not long into this thrusting spectacle, Sarah's head began bumping on the side of the elevator.

"I'm sorry, I'm sorry," Tim said.

"Don't worry," Sarah said breathlessly. "You're doing good." She closed her eyes and returned her thoughts to the first time she and Jack had sex with CJ. She had a favorite moment where one man was thrusting from the front and the other thrusting from behind, both on the verge of orgasm. A moment later, Sarah firmly held on to the railing as an orgasm rolled through her. Her heavy breathing slowly turned into a suppressed laugh as the elevator started moving again. Sarah did her best to avoid making noise as the floors ticked by with Tim thrusting wildly. She didn't want to distract him, but all she could see in her mind's eye was the elevator doors opening to some poor old couple who would be emotionally scarred for life. She began to press back into each thrust.

"You need to be quick, Tim," she urged.

The floors were counting by quickly. Twentieth floor. Ding. Thirtieth floor. Ding. Fortieth floor. Ding. "You only have twenty more," Sarah said. Finally, she reached between her legs and firmly squeezed his balls. Sarah could feel them convulse as Tim let out a loud moan which lasted for three or four thrusts. He held them together until the elevator stopped at Sarah's floor. She gently pulled away from Tim, lifted her underwear, and lowered her skirt. When the doors opened, Jack and CJ were standing with their arms over each other's shoulders, each with a smiling look of anticipation.

"Well?" Jack said as they stepped off the elevator.

Tim just smiled and shrugged his shoulders.

Jack pleaded with Sarah. "Come on, yes or no?"

Sarah smiled, grabbed Tim's hand, and pulled him close.

"Somehow," she said as she kissed him. "Against all odds," she said as she kissed him again. "Yes." With that, she gave Tim a long, passionate kiss. Jack and CJ began dancing around, cheering, and high-fiving each other, including Tim.

"Thank you, Tim," Sarah said. "And sorry about the face."

"The pleasure was all mine," Tim said, kissing her hand. "Face and all."

"Face?" Jack asked.

"I'll tell you later," Sarah said as she walked back onto the elevator. "Now, about that Sushi?"

CHAPTER TWENTY-FOUR

*O*f all the fantasies on Sarah's list, the current one proved the hardest for Jack to arrange. Sarah wanted to make love with a man who couldn't speak English. It didn't matter what language he did speak, as long as he couldn't use words to communicate with her.

Sarah and Jack both knew that there was a risk that this fantasy would work better in her head than it did in reality. She expected uncomfortable and awkward moments, but that was part of the excitement. The risk was that if those moments reached a tipping point, her experience would quickly devolve from an exciting evening fulfilling a fantasy to simply a botched attempt to have sex with a stranger.

Jack struck out with his usually dependable channels for supplying men for the fantasies: Brooke, the club, and the internet. He never imagined it would be so hard to find an appropriate man to make love with his wife.

"Hello, goodbye, please, and thank you," Sarah had said. "Not a word more."

Ironically, it was CJ who discovered someone who met those requirements. He was the cousin of the bartender at

CJ's favorite Italian restaurant. The bartender was privy to CJ's lifestyle, and one night, while at the bar, CJ asked him if he had any attractive friends who couldn't speak English. As it happened, the bartender had a cousin, Alessandro, visiting from a small industrial town in rural Italy, a part of the world that saw little value in learning English. So he never bothered to try.

When the bartender first explained to Alessandro what they were asking of him, he thought they were playing a prank. When he realized they weren't kidding, he assumed Sarah was ugly. But when Jack met them at the restaurant and showed Alessandro a picture, he figured he had nothing to lose.

Later that weekend, when Sarah saw Jack greet Alessandro at the door of their suite, she immediately questioned whether or not this was a good idea.

"Buonasera," Alessandro said, stepping into the suite.

"Buonasera," Jack parroted back, hoping that he just said hello.

Sarah nervously stepped forward to greet Alessandro as he stepped close and kissed her on both cheeks. Sarah stepped back and smiled. Then she looked at Jack and smiled. Then all three looked back and forth at each other and smiled.

Finally, Sarah broke up the awkward staring contest. "Champagne, please?"

"On it," Jack said, gesturing for Alessandro to sit on the couch.

"Jack, what was I thinking?" Sarah laughed. "I literally don't know what to say to him."

"Babe, I'll let you in on a little secret; as you requested, it doesn't matter what you say. He won't understand a word of it."

"Then what the hell am I supposed to do?"

Jack laughed as he removed the foil off the champagne bottle. "Hell if I know. It wasn't my fantasy."

"Thanks. You're being very helpful."

Jack laughed. "What do you think I can do to help?" With that, he sent the cork flying across the suite. "How did it go in your fantasy?"

"In my fantasy, he just grabs me and takes me."

Alessandro sat looking back and forth between them, clearly not knowing what to do either. Jack poured three glasses of champagne and passed them around. Alessandro held his glass up to toast.

"Cheers," Jack said.

"Salute," Alessandro said.

"Salute?" Sarah repeated.

Alessandro smiled and turned to Sarah. "Sì. Salute."

"Salute. Cheers," Sarah repeated. She took a sip of champagne. "Jack, now what?"

"Babe, if I were you, I would create an environment that invited him to behave like he would in your fantasy."

"Damn, I didn't expect to have trouble understanding *you* through all this."

"Take off some clothes. Turn down the lights. Climb onto the bed. Create an environment where Alessandro can't help but take you."

Alessandro set his champagne down on the coffee table and stood up. "Tutto bene? Devo andare via?"

Sarah quickly stood up as well. "I'm sorry, I don't understand."

Alessandro patted himself on the chest and pointed to the suite's door. "Devo andare via?"

"No, no. Everything is fine," Sarah said as she patted the couch.

"Sei Bellissima," Alessandro said, looking into her eyes.

Sarah just smiled and shook her head.

Alessandro took another sip of champagne. "Quindi, da quanto ho capito, tuo marito rimarrà qui a guardarci?"

"I have no idea what you are saying," Sarah said. Turning to Jack, she added, "What was I thinking?"

Jack leaned back in a seat at the end of the couch. "Do you want to have sex with him?"

"Are you kidding? He's gorgeous."

"Well, it appears to me that, unlike your fantasy, you will have to be the aggressor here. At least, in the spirit of making the first move."

Sarah let out a deep breath and stood up from her chair. She walked over and stood in front of Alessandro. When he started to stand, Sarah put her hand on his shoulder and kept him seated.

"May I kiss you?" she asked, even though she knew he wouldn't understand the words she used.

"Non capisco," he said.

"Geronimo, Babe," Jack said, taking a sip of champagne.

Sarah took Alessandro's champagne flute and placed it on the end table. Looking at Jack, she winked as she straddled Alessandro on the couch, placing a knee on either side of his lap. "Kiss," Sarah said softly as she leaned forward and kissed Alessandro.

Sarah and Alessandro proceeded to kiss passionately. She squeezed her thighs against his and began to rub her pelvis against him.

"Oh, dio, sei così calda..." Alessandro said between kisses. "Posso spogliarti?"

"I don't understand," Sarah replied, kissing him deeply.

Alessandro held her firmly by both shoulders and pushed her away. "Posso spogliarti?" he said as he slowly unbuttoned the top button on her shirt. He paused before repeating himself as he unbuttoned the second button. "Posso spogliarti."

"Yes, yes," Sarah said as she began to unbutton his shirt. When Alessandro unbuttoned the last button of her shirt, she stood up and let it fall to the floor. Alessandro took off his shirt as Sarah removed her shoes, slipped out of her skirt, and dropped to her knees at his feet. He leaned forward and kissed her as she removed his socks and shoes. He continued to kiss her as she unbuckled his pants. With his pants unfastened, he stood up and let them drop to the floor. Sarah jumped into his arms and straddled him with her legs.

"The bed," she said quickly. "The bed."

"Non capisco," Alessandro said, starting to kiss her again.

"The bed, the bed," Sarah said, pointing into the bedroom.

"Ah, sì, la camera da letto," he said as he walked towards the bedroom.

"Did he just say something about a camera?" Sarah asked Jack, kissing Alessandro along the way to the bedroom.

"I don't think that is a camera in his underwear, so I believe you are safe," Jack said.

Alessandro gently laid Sarah on the bed and climbed up next to her. He curled her silky brown hair up over her ear and kissed her neck. "Sei una donna molto bella," Alessandro said.

Jack walked over and sat down in a chair next to the bed with the champagne flute and the bottle of champagne in hand. Sarah smiled at him when she saw him taking a seat.

"This is more the fantasy, Jack," Sarah said. "I have no idea what he keeps saying, but I love it."

"I believe that was the point," Jack said, returning Sarah's smile.

"He could be calling me a filthy little whore for all I know, but it sounds so sexy. "

Alessandro deftly removed her bra and began to kiss his way down to her nipples. When he gently pulled Sarah's underwear aside and slipped a finger inside her, he let out a long groan. "Oh, vedo che sei già bagnata, tesoro...."

"He is quite talented with his fingers."

Jack took a sip of champagne. "Don't tell me. Tell him."

"He won't understand."

"Oh yes, he will."

Alessandro quickly removed her panties and returned to gently fingering her while he kissed and licked her nipples.

"Alessandro, your fingers are magical."

"Non capisco," he said before quickly returning his lips to her breasts.

Sarah reached down and gently placed her hand on his and moved back and forth with his hand. "Good," she said.

"Buona?" he asked.

"Sì. Buona!" she replied.

Alessandro looked up and smiled. "Hai un preservativo?"

Sarah smiled down at him and laughed. "I have no idea what you are saying."

"Un preservativo?"

"Alessandro, I've got nothing," she said.

"Ehm... Durex?"

"Ah," Sarah said. "A condom." She turned to face Jack. "Hey, would you be so kind as to get this man a condom so he can make love with your wife?"

"Happy to play my role," Jack said. He turned and opened the nightstand drawer and pulled out a box of condoms. Alessandro rolled off the side of the bed and accepted the box from Jack.

"Grazie."

Sarah rolled over to the side of the bed and lay on her stomach. She pulled Alessandro's underwear down, revealing an extremely erect penis. She grabbed his cock at its base and pulled it towards her as she plunged her lips down around it.

"Santa madre di Dio e del cielo," Alessandro said as he

struggled to open the box of condoms. After a couple of minutes, Alessandro gave up on the box, lowering it in one hand by his side while placing his other hand on the back of Sarah's head. "Oh, dio, sei così calda..." he said in little more than a whisper.

Sarah had no idea what Alessandro was saying, but his voice made it clear that what she was doing to him needed no words.

"You might want to be careful," Jack said.

Sarah ignored Jack's warning. If anything, she pulled and sucked Alessandro even harder.

Alessandro dropped the condoms on the bed and gently took Sarah's head with both hands. "Madre di Dio," is what he repeated over and over. A moment later the "Madre di Dio" changed to an urgent "Per favore fermata." He did his best to pull his cock from Sarah's mouth, but she wasn't giving it up. "Per favore fermata!" he shouted. "Vengo!"

"I told you," Jack replied.

"Vengo! Vengo! Vengo!" he said as his muscles bent him at the waist in contraction. "Sei così calda," Alessandro said, trying to catch his breath.

Sarah took his cock out of her mouth, swallowed, and kissed his stomach. She leaned back and smiled up at him. "You vengo? Really?" she said, feigning a sad face.

Alessandro's eye went wide as he looked back and forth between Sarah and Jack. "Le ho richiesto di smettere," he protested to Jack. "Ti ho richiesto di fermarti," he protested to Sarah.

Sarah just smiled, laid back in the middle of the bed, and slowly spread her legs.

Alessandro held up his flaccid penis to show Sarah that it was broken. "Stupido. Stupido. Stupido," he said, shaking his soft dick each time he said the word.

"Jack?" Sarah asked with a soft, sultry voice as she began to rub herself.

"Yes?"

"Is your penis stupido at the moment?"

"Fuck no," Jack said, sending his clothes flying like they were in a tornado. "Excuse me," he said as he walked past Alessandro.

Alessandro looked at the scene like a disappointed child. Jack climbed between Sarah's legs and quickly entered her. Sarah smiled when Alessandro started to pull on his underwear.

"Alessandro, no!" Sarah said without taking her eyes off Jack. "Sit. Sit," she said, pointing to the chair by the bed.

"Good lord, you are so freakin' wet," Jack said. "I don't ever remember you being this wet," he said without breaking stride.

"That's what you said when I was with CJ," she replied.

"Well," Jack said, "it was true at the time. And it's true now." He looked over and saw Alessandro rubbing himself like a madman, apparently doing his best to fix "stupido." Jack let out a small chuckle. "Sarah, you might want to help out Alessandro before he breaks that thing off."

Sarah looked over and immediately shared Jack's concern. She had never seen anyone rub a cock like he was rubbing. "You don't mind?" she said to Jack.

"Well, let's be clear; I don't mind you helping him, but not if I have to stop for you to do it," he said.

Sarah looked over at Alessandro and smiled. "Alessandro, let me help," she said.

"Non capisco," Alessandro said without slowing down the abuse he was inflicting upon his cock.

"Let me help," she said again slowly. She pointed at Alessandro's cock, held up her finger, and slid it into her mouth.

Jack shifted to a kneeling position in front of Sarah and lifted her legs over his shoulders. Alessandro sprung from the chair to the side of the bed, standing with one foot on the floor and one knee on the bed. He hesitantly approached Sarah's mouth with his flaccid cock in hand with a timid smile. Sarah smiled as she guided him towards her mouth. She began to barely lick the head of his cock like a lollipop.

"Stupido," she said with a smile as she once again took Alessandro into her mouth.

Watching his wife give another man a blowjob was one of those out-of-body experiences for Jack. It was so hard for him to imagine that this was the same woman he had spent years and years having adequate missionary position sex with. The more he heard the sucking sounds she was making, the harder Jack thrust. And the harder Jack thrust, the more sucking noises he heard.

"Holy shit, Jack. I'm about to come," Sarah said as she continued to rub Alessandro. "What is it about having a dick in my mouth while you fuck me that makes me come so easily?"

Jack was too busy focusing on fucking his wife to ponder one of the great mysteries of group sex. He was about to come himself.

"What is it about watching you suck another man's cock that makes me come so easily?"

Sarah laughed.

"And on that note...." Jack said.

"Not inside me," Sarah quickly said as she took Alessandro back into her mouth.

"What?" Jack asked, a little panicked.

"Don't come inside me," Sarah quickly said as she finally gave in to her own orgasm. She let out a long moan.

Jack pulled out and came on her stomach.

Sarah laid still as she tried to catch her breath. "Look,

Jack," she said when she realized Alessandro had an erection. "Much better," Sarah said, smiling up at Alessandro. She picked up the box of condoms off the bed, quickly opened the top, and handed one to Alessandro. "Let's try this again," she said.

Jack grabbed a warm washcloth and returned to clean Sarah's stomach. Then he grabbed the bottle of champagne and took a seat in the chair by the bed. Alessandro quickly climbed on the bed and positioned himself between Sarah's legs. The whole time he opened the condom wrapper and put the condom on, he looked down at Sarah and talked. Jack leaned back and sipped his champagne. He couldn't help but smile as Alessandro made love with his wife. Sarah was right. It didn't matter what Alessandro was saying. Every word he spoke painted a picture that Sarah was the sexiest, most beautiful woman in the world and that there was nowhere he would rather be.

CHAPTER TWENTY-FIVE

Over breakfast, Jack offered to fulfill any fantasy Sarah wanted–on the list or not–for her birthday. Her answer was not at all what he expected.

"I want to stay in, Jack."

"Seriously?"

"Seriously. I'll check with Mom to see if she will keep Colin at her place."

"Well, it's your birthday," Jack said. "Do you want me to make reservations at Garibaldi's?"

"No. I want to do something different this year. I want you and I to cook dinner together," Sarah said. "I think it'll be fun."

"Oh lord," Jack said. "And what exactly did you have in mind?"

"I want to make ravioli. From scratch."

"We don't have a pasta machine."

"Well then, I guess you know what to get me for my birthday."

Jack looked up from the Wall Street Journal with a scowl. "Do you remember when we tried to hang wallpaper in our first apartment? I believe you had seen someone do it on television, and you thought it 'would be fun.'"

"It was fun," she exclaimed.

"Sarah, we almost got divorced three weeks into our marriage."

Sarah stood up from the kitchen table and began clearing plates. "Don't you remember how much we laughed?"

"Whatever laughter there may have been came after quite a few tears."

"Well, I'm not asking you to hang any more wallpaper. I just want to roll a little pasta. Besides, it's my birthday."

Jack got up from the table, walked into the kitchen, and kissed her. "If homemade pasta is what you want, then homemade pasta you'll get."

Sarah's mother agreed to watch Colin, though she didn't believe that they were staying home to cook a meal together. Maureen's imagination went straight to a swinger birthday party.

Sarah handled the menu and the grocery shopping while Jack bought the pasta maker and the wine. After watching several videos on YouTube trying to learn how to make ravioli, Jack put their odds of pulling it off at no better than fifty-fifty.

With the wallpaper hanging episode fresh in their minds, Jack and Sarah decided they needed some ground rules. First: they had to dress up as they would if they were going out on a date. Second: no tears. Third: they could start over as many times as was necessary, but they eventually had to eat whatever they cooked. And fourth, they had to play High-Low during dinner, a game they played with Colin where each person shared the best and the worst part of their day. In this case, however, Sarah wanted to share what they each considered their favorite and least favorite part of their efforts to fulfill her fantasies.

Though cooking dinner took about three times longer than expected and covered everything and everyone in the kitchen in flour, they pulled it off. And unlike their wallpaper fiasco, no tears were shed in the process. Instead, they had a great time making mistakes, starting over, and drinking too much wine. As they sat there eating the results of their shared victory, butternut squash ravioli and grilled asparagus, Sarah leaned back and smiled.

"I know two things for sure about this meal," she said.

"And those are?" Jack asked.

"First of all, it was fantastic."

"Couldn't agree more. And the second?"

"I can almost guarantee we can never make it this good again," she laughed.

"I think that we could do even better with practice."

"Nope," Sarah said. "Pack it up, send it back. We hit perfection. Nowhere to go from here but down."

"Fine," Jack said. "Now, High-Low. What was your favorite part of the fantasies we have covered so far?"

"That's easy," Sarah said, taking a sip of her wine. "The anticipation."

"Seriously?"

"Seriously."

"Not CJ's ridiculous cock, or Alessandro's talented fingers, or having an entire playroom watch you make love with your boyfriend?"

"Nope. It's the excitement of not knowing what to expect. It's the anticipation of knowing that something new and potentially amazing might happen."

"And it feels wrong?"

"Well, there is that," she said with a smile.

Jack took another bite of ravioli. "And your least favorite?"

"What it has done to my relationship with my mother."

"Ugh."

"Yeah, agreed. And it's not like I can sit down and explain it to her. Honestly, Jack, if you told me a year ago that she or my sister Ashley were out behaving like this, there is zero chance I would have understood. I would have been mortified."

Jack reached across the table and rubbed her hand. "Regrets?"

Sarah thought for a moment before answering. "The only regret I have is that I can't have both. Live the way I choose to live, doing the things I want to do...yet keep the relationship I had with my mom."

"I'm afraid that's asking a lot."

"I know. But a woman can dream." Sarah took her foot out of her high-heeled shoe and gently ran it up to Jack's inner thigh. "So, what is your favorite part of this whole endeavor?" she asked as she rubbed Jack's growing erection.

Jack slumped a little in his chair to give Sarah better access as he shared his thoughts. "My favorite part is watching how horny you get."

"That's your favorite part?"

"Absolutely."

"It's not CJ's ridiculous cock, or Alessandro's talented fingers, or having an entire playroom watch you make love with your girlfriend?" she parroted back to Jack in a soft, cute voice.

"Nope. It's simply watching how horny you get."

"Jack, I get horny a lot. You just rarely noticed."

"That's not true. There is I-would-enjoy-an-orgasm-right-now horny. And there is if-I-don't-have-an-orgasm-right-now-I-will-explode horny. And the former comes from seeing me and thinking that you could always sleep with me for the thousandth time. The latter comes from CJ's ridiculous cock, or Alessandro's talented fingers, or having an entire playroom watch you make love with your boyfriend."

Sarah smiled at Jack and winked. "Well, why don't you come here and fuck me on the island and let's make it a thousand and one." She got up from her chair, stepped out of her underwear, and hopped up on the kitchen island.

"I mean, I already gave you a pasta maker, but...if this is what you want," Jack said as he stood and walked between her legs. He kissed her passionately as she furiously tried to unbuckle his belt and take off his pants. A moment after he entered her, the doorbell rang.

"Are you fucking kidding me?" Sarah asked.

"Are you expecting anyone?" Jack asked.

"No."

"Forget it. They'll go away," Jack said, laughing as he continued to thrust. "Jack, you need to see who it is," Sarah said.

"If it's important, whoever it is will still be there in a few minutes," Jack said, still thrusting and laughing.

Sarah's cell phone on the counter rang, and she was close enough to read the caller ID. It said: Mom. "Jack, stop." Sarah hopped down off the counter and grabbed the phone.

"Mom? Is everything okay?"

"I thought you were staying home to cook dinner," she said, completely ignoring Sarah's question.

"We did, Mom."

"Then where did you go?"

"Mom, are you the one ringing the doorbell?"

There was a long pause before she spoke. "Yes. Are you home?"

"Yes. One second and I'll let you in."

Sarah turned to Jack before walking to the front door. "You might want to put that away," she said, nodding to his sad erection.

Sarah turned on the front porch light and opened the door. "Is everything okay?"

"Colin said he was scared and wanted to come home," Maureen said, holding the hand of the sleepy child by her side.

"Mom, Colin has stayed with you a hundred times, and this is the night he gets scared and wants to come home?"

"I'm not sure what you want me to tell you."

"Just come in," Sarah said, swooping Colin up in her arms.

Maureen followed her into the house, looking as if she was afraid people or sights might jump out and surprise her. "You look awfully dressed up for having not gone out."

Sarah walked into the kitchen and handed Colin to Jack. "Hello, Maureen," Jack said.

"Hello," she replied.

Jack carried Colin to his bedroom to put him to sleep.

"It was a part of my deal with Jack. We decided to dress up for dinner."

"You expect me to believe that you went to all the trouble to get dressed up just so that you could eat at home?"

"Mom, I don't expect you to believe anything I say these days. But it's the truth." Sarah looked down at some of the leftover ravioli. "Would you like to try some? It's actually quite good."

"No," she said. "I need to be going."

Jack walked back into the room as Maureen was walking out.

"Leaving already?" he asked.

"Yes. Sorry for interrupting your special evening," Maureen said with dripping sarcasm.

"Well, thanks for watching Colin for us so that we could enjoy it," Sarah said with equally dripping sarcasm.

Maureen walked herself out and let the front door slam.

Sarah and Jack exchanged a look of frustration. "Who knew your mother would be such a cock block?"

Sarah walked to the front door and watched her mother

get in the car and drive away. Jack walked up behind Sarah and started to rub her shoulders.

"Why does my sex life have any effect on my relationship with my mother?"

"I think it's fair to say that recent events have changed how she thinks about your sex life."

Sarah turned around and faced Jack. "Why would she think about my sex life at all?"

"Babe, I don't think she sits around pondering it, but you have to admit that seeing that dress and Captain Lifelike didn't give her much choice."

"Captain Lifelike? Thanks, Jack. Like I didn't feel like crap already."

Jack kissed her and turned to walk back into the kitchen, holding her hand along the way. He stopped in front of the island where they were when Maureen interrupted them. "Hop up here. Captain Adequate has a job to finish."

Sarah laughed. "And Colin?"

"That child is so tired he might not wake up until Monday."

Sarah smiled, hopped up on the island, and pulled Jack close. She stroked him a couple of times before guiding him inside her. "You say we've made love a thousand times."

"Well, that was to make a point of how boring and routine having sex with me is," he said with a smile.

Sarah kissed him and grabbed his hips to slow his thrust to almost a crawl. She guided him slowly in and out, pausing briefly before doing it again. "You feel different inside me."

Jack laughed. "Nope, same old me."

"No, I mean that after I am with someone else, you feel different the next time you and I make love."

"That doesn't make any sense."

"I didn't say I could explain it. But you do. Different, yet familiar. It's like coming back home. Safe. Like home base."

Jack kissed her. His pace quickened, but he didn't stop kissing her. When he noticed small tears fall from Sarah's eyes, he stopped thrusting. "What's the matter?"

"Don't stop," Sarah said as she pulled him into her. "Happy tears. Happy tears," she said, deeply kissing him.

Jack held her tight as they continued to make love. There were things to be concerned with, and some decisions would need to be made. But not tonight. Tonight they were together, safe at home.

CHAPTER TWENTY-SIX

Jack had invested a great deal of time looking for someone who met Sarah's requirements for her younger man fantasy. She struggled to verbalize what excited her about it, but she was pretty specific with what she wanted. She asked Jack to find someone in his early twenties who carried himself with a maturity well beyond his years yet still possessed an air of inexperience.

Jack created a profile for Sarah on a website that matched young men with cougars. He posted a handful of photos, though none contained her face or nudity. When Jack asked her to approve the profile before he made it live, Sarah couldn't help but laugh. The profile name was perfect: Mrs. 26544, their membership number at Lux.

Jack wasn't sure what to expect, given that what they were requesting was different than the norm for this website. The profile made it clear that they were interested in a one-time interlude that would include Jack. Most people on this site were looking to develop an ongoing, one-on-one relationship. But he didn't have any better ideas. He could have asked

Brooke, but he knew Sarah thought they had gone to the Broke well one too many times already. With Sarah's approval, he hit publish and sat back to wait.

He was amazed at how quickly the messages flowed in. It was easy for Jack to eliminate over ninety percent of them based on age, looks, or the tone they took in the messages. For example, the poetic words from YungHungMeat69 did nothing to inspire Jack to reply: "As long as I don't see your old man's dick."

In the end, Jack reached out to four. In each case, they were good-looking kids who appeared to be both respectful and, as indicated on their profiles, they had previous experience with women on the site. After several exchanges with each, Jack decided on Brandon, a twenty-three-year-old senior at a nearby college. Brandon had a brief relationship the previous summer with a woman who had moved away, but she couldn't say enough about how respectful he was in her reviews. Jack thought he was perfect for Sarah.

Sitting at their favorite bar awaiting his arrival, Sarah sat nervously inspecting every face that walked by.

"Relax," Jack suggested, though he, too, was a little nervous.

"I'm trying," she said while she continued to scan the room.

About five minutes after the appointed hour, what looked like a handsome teenager walked into the bar and took a seat three stools down from them. He glanced their way several times before finally turning to face them.

"This will sound strange if I get it wrong, but are you Mrs. 26544?"

Sarah did a double-take with Jack.

"Brandon?" she asked.

"Yes," he said as he stood to greet them.

Jack shook his hand, but it was apparent that this Brandon was not the young man in the photos. "I'm Jack, and this is my wife, Sarah," he said, immediately regretting it as soon as the words left his mouth.

"Hello," he said, shaking Sarah's hand. Brandon turned to the bartender and said, "Can I get a Budweiser, please?"

The bartender walked over and looked at the young man. Then he looked at Jack to assess how important this kid was to the couple, who were clearly important to the general manager. Jack just shrugged his shoulders.

"Can I see your ID, please?" the bartender asked.

"Sure," he said, removing his wallet from his back pocket.

Sarah couldn't wait any longer. "I don't want to offend you, Brandon, but you don't look like your pictures, and you don't look twenty-three."

Brandon gave her an annoyed look as he removed his license from his wallet and handed it to the bartender.

"You may look like your pictures, kid, but this ain't one of them," the bartender said without emotion.

"May I see that, please?" Sarah asked the bartender.

The bartender handed it across to Sarah without hesitation. Sarah looked at the photo and immediately recognized the young man from the website profile. She could see a resemblance, but it was clearly not the ID of the young man in front of them. Sarah looked up at the boy and gave him a gentle smile. "Your brother?" she asked.

The young man hung his head. "Yeah."

Sarah reached out and touched his sleeve. "What's your name?"

"Ethan," the young man said sheepishly.

"How old are you, Ethan?"

"Eighteen," he said.

"Eighteen?" Sarah asked rhetorically.

"Yeah, but I'll be nineteen in a few weeks," he said, looking up with a reassuring smile.

Sarah looked to Jack for some assistance.

"Ethan, would you like something to drink...other than alcohol?" Jack asked.

"Sure, I guess. Coke would be great."

Jack looked up at the bartender, but he had already started to pour the young man a drink. When he returned with the glass, he handed it to Ethan with a, "Here you go, kid."

Jack tried to give the bartender a dirty look, but he couldn't help but smile. The bartender shrugged his shoulders and went about his business.

Picking up his drink, Jack suggested finding a place where they might have a little more privacy. "What were you thinking?" Jack asked Ethan once they were all seated at a table off in the corner.

"My brother found a match on the website last year, and he had the summer of his life."

"Ethan, there is a big difference between eighteen and twenty-three," Jack said.

"Not really," Ethan said, trying to convince them.

"Yes, Ethan, there is."

"I'm not a virgin if that's what you mean," he said forcefully.

"Oh my god," Sarah said as she turned in her seat as if to remove herself from the conversation.

"Well, I'm not," Ethan said in her direction.

They sat there in silence for a moment, each lost in thought. "Does your brother know you are doing this?" Jack asked.

Ethan hung his head.

"Ethan?"

"No. Brandon is going to school in France for the summer.

I guessed his password one day, so I could see some of the pictures women had sent him."

Sarah had heard enough. "Do you know how wrong that is, Ethan? That is an invasion of his privacy. For that matter, of the women as well."

"I know," he said quickly. "But I figured if they were willing to post pictures of themselves on the internet, what did it matter if I looked at them?"

"Ethan, if women sent those pictures in messages to your brother, they weren't for the world to see. They were for your brother to see."

"You're right. I'm sorry."

"So, how did you go from looking at pictures to pretending that you are your brother?" Jack asked.

"One day, while I was looking through pictures, a new message came in from a woman who had just joined the website. I didn't even think about it. I just answered it how I thought my brother would."

"And?"

"And the next thing I know, I'm carrying on lengthy text exchanges with a recently divorced forty-two-year-old who was at her wit's end with her eighteen-year-old son."

Jack and Sarah both let out a laugh in unison.

"Yes," Ethan said. "I saw the irony as well."

Jack finished his drink and stood up. "I'm going to grab another drink. Ethan, I'm trusting you will behave while I'm gone?"

"Yes, I promise."

Jack smiled at Sarah and walked over to the bar.

Ethan turned his chair to face Sarah squarely. "We can still have sex if you want," he offered with a great deal of hope in his voice.

Sarah reached out and touched his hand. "No, Ethan. We can't."

"But why? Is it because of him?" Ethan asked, nodding in Jack's direction.

"No. It is because of you."

"Because I lied?" he asked.

"Partially," Sarah said. "But honestly, you're not what I am looking for."

"So it's because I am not as good-looking as my brother?" he asked, looking down at his drink.

"No, Ethan, I think you are very handsome. But…" Sarah said, hesitating as she struggled to find the right words. "Eighteen is not what I was looking for."

"I understand," he said. "But if I was older, I would be good-looking enough for you?"

"Yes, Ethan. You would be good-looking enough for me," she said with a smile.

"Thanks," he said. "And for what it's worth, I think you're really good-looking. Even without your face in them, I've used your pictures several times to…."

"Okay, Ethan," Sarah said, quickly interrupting. "I get the picture."

Ethan sat quietly for a moment. "I know you thought you were sending those pictures to Brandon, but would it be okay if I kept them, for, you know?"

Sarah couldn't help but smile. "Yes, Ethan, that's fine. I want you to have them."

"Thanks," he said with a grin.

Jack could see Ethan beaming as he walked up. "Everything good?" he asked.

"Yeah, Jack. We're good," Sarah said. Turning back to Ethan, she continued. "I saw on your driver's license that you live in Wyckoff."

"Yeah."

"How are you getting home?" she asked.

"I'll walk to Penn Station, take the train to Ridgewood,

and then call a friend to come to pick me up."

Sarah looked over at Jack with almost a dirty look. Jack rolled his eyes.

"Fine," he said. Pulling his phone out, he dialed a number. "Hey, Yuri? I know we said we weren't going to need you tonight, but is there any chance you can make a quick trip from the hotel to Jersey for me? Wykoff. One way. It's a long story. Thanks."

Jack looked up at Ethan. "Okay, kid, I've arranged a ride for you, but under two conditions."

"Okay?" Ethan asked.

"First, you do not discuss this with our driver or your friends, clear?"

"Clear."

"And second, ask the driver to drop you off a couple of blocks from your house. I don't want your mother asking you what you were doing in a limo."

"A limo?"

"Yes, a limo. Now was I clear?

"Yes. Don't discuss this with anyone, and walk the last couple of blocks."

Sarah stood up and guided Ethan out of his chair by his hand. Giving him a long hug, she said, "Don't be so quick to grow up, Ethan. You will have plenty of time for amazing summers when you are a little older."

As Sarah slowly stepped back from Ethan's embrace, she saw his rather large erection pressing against his pants. "Are you kidding me?" Sarah asked in disbelief.

"I'm sorry. I can't help it," Ethan pleaded.

Jack started to laugh.

"It's not funny, Jack," Sarah said, clearly annoyed.

As Jack continued to laugh, Ethan slowly began to laugh with him.

"Listen, you two. It's not funny," Sarah said, though she also began to laugh.

Jack grabbed her hand. "It's a little funny."

Sarah sat down and turned away from the boys. "Fine, Jack. Let's see how funny it is when I make you chaperone Ethan and his erection to Jersey," Sarah said, lifting her drink. "Now, that would be funny."

CHAPTER TWENTY-SEVEN

Sarah had asked Jack if they could put the fantasy efforts on hold for the evening. She wanted to dance and have fun without any objectives or expectations. If the opportunity to misbehave presented itself, she promised she would welcome that as well.

When they first arrived at Lux, they saw CJ with his friend, Barbara, from Chicago. Sarah's first impression was how pretty she was, followed immediately by how tall she was. While introductions were made, Sarah wondered if CJ had told Barbara about his time with her and Jack. Not long into the evening, Barbara disappeared into the back with an attractive younger white couple she had planned to meet.

"Does she know about us?" Sarah asked CJ once Barbara was gone.

"What is there to know about us?" CJ asked.

"You know, that we *had sex*."

CJ smiled. "I don't share my business with anyone, Sarah. I'm certainly not going to share yours."

"Oh," Sarah replied.

"But to answer what I believe was the point of your question, yes, I'm sure she knows we *had sex*," he said with a similar tone as Sarah had used earlier.

"Are you making fun of me?" Sarah asked, slapping him on the leg.

"Yeah, a little," CJ said with a smile

CJ looked over at Jack and said it one more time. "We *had sex*."

"Well, if you didn't tell her, how does she know?" Sarah asked.

"Because it is written all over your face," Jack chimed in.

"What he said," CJ said, pointing at Jack.

"No, it's not," Sarah protested.

"Yes, it is," Jack laughed. "Here, watch this. Excuse me, sir?" Jack said to a shirtless, fifty-something-year-old man in a pair of pajama bottoms—clearly sneaking into the front room to grab a quick bite from the buffet before returning to the back room. "Do you think this beautiful woman here has ever had sex with this distinguished gentleman?"

The man stopped and looked at Jack. "I don't even know them."

"No, I just want you to look at her face. Does she look like she has *had sex* with him?"

The man, fairly drunk, began to protest. "How am I supposed to know..." he said as he looked up at Sarah. "Oh, strike that. Yeah, she fucked him," he said as he turned to hurry off to the back rooms. "And she liked it. A lot," he said over his shoulder.

Jack beamed at Sarah.

Sarah glared back with a playful grin. "See if I ever *have sex* with either of you again."

"I'll risk it," Jack said.

"Fine," Sarah said, grabbing CJ and heading for the dance floor. "Then you risk sitting alone and watching."

"Wouldn't be the first time!" Jack yelled after her with a smile.

Jack was grateful that CJ was there to assist in satisfying Sarah's thirst to dance. They took turns dancing with her, and they even danced to a few songs together. After about an hour, Jack went to the bathroom, CJ went to get a round of drinks, and Sarah dropped down into a chair at a table just off the dance floor. Waiting for the men to return, she noticed a familiar face walking in her direction.

"Monica?" Sarah asked, standing up from her chair. "What are you doing here?"

"What am I doing here?" Monica asked. "What are you doing here?"

"I'm here with Jack."

"First a threesome. Now a sex club?" Monica asked without any sign of judgment.

"Actually, the sex club was first. Then the threesome," Sarah clarified.

"Well, either way, we need to talk. Quickly," Monica said.

"No shit. When Jack sees you, he will assume I told you about this place."

"It's worse than that," Monica said, stopping short of explaining why.

"What are you talking about?"

"I may have made a mistake."

"You mean worse than Jack thinking I told you about the club?"

"That depends on you."

"Monica? What are you not telling me?"

Before Monica could answer, Sarah saw Jack walking back from the bathroom with Marcus by his side.

"Hey, babe, look who I ran into," Jack said before realizing who it was standing next to his wife. "Monica?" he said in disbelief.

"Hey, Jack," Monica said with a forced smile.

Jack immediately looked at Sarah. "You told her about the club?"

"No, Jack," she said, hanging her head. "Not about the club."

Marcus walked over and gave Sarah a quick kiss. "You guys know each other?" he asked, looking at Monica.

Sarah was confused until that moment. Then reality struck.

Monica handed Marcus the drink that she was holding for him while he was in the bathroom. "Yup," she said. "Sarah's my best friend."

"Oh," Marcus said, giving Monica a somewhat stern look.

CJ arrived with a handful of drinks and passed them out to Sarah and Jack.

Sarah gestured to Marcus. "Marcus, this is CJ. CJ, this is Marcus."

Marcus leaned in and shook CJ's hand. "Nice to meet you."

"Pleasure's mine," CJ said.

"Can someone please explain to me what is going on?" Jack asked.

"What did I miss?" CJ asked.

When nobody answered, Jack looked at Sarah. "Sarah?"

Sarah looked up at Jack. "I'm not a hundred percent sure."

Jack was shaking his head. "Can you please tell me the part you are sure of?"

"I told Monica about our evening with Marcus...and about the store."

Jack took a step back and looked at the ground. He was trying his best not to let his anger show in how he spoke: "I thought we agreed not to tell a soul about this part of our life?"

"We did, Jack."

"And?"

"I had to speak with someone, and it just came out," Sarah said.

"So, it just came out?"

"You had to be there."

"I assume you told her about sleeping with CJ as well?" Jack asked.

"As well?" Monica chimed in. "You told me you and Marcus didn't sleep together."

"We didn't," Sarah said.

"But you did sleep with CJ?" Marcus asked.

"Yes," she said. "Did you sleep with Monica?" she snapped, looking directly at Marcus.

"Sarah," Jack interrupted. "That's none of your business."

Sarah sat down at their table. "You're right," she said. Looking up at Marcus, she added, "I'm sorry."

CJ looked over at Marcus. "Hey, you care to join me for a drink at the bar?"

Marcus stood up and kissed Monica's hand. "I'll be at the bar when you all finish whatever this is."

Jack gave Sarah a dirty look, grabbed his drink, and fell in step behind the other men. "Wait on me. I think I've heard enough over here."

Sarah gave Monica a dirty look as she took a seat at their table. Monica forced herself to sit in a chair next to Sarah. After a few long minutes of silence, Monica finally spoke. "You said you would give me his number."

"I did," Sarah admitted.

"I thought that meant you wouldn't mind."

Sarah hesitated for a moment. "I don't," she finally said.

Monica laughed. "Yes, Sarah, you do."

Sarah was running her finger around the rim of her glass. "Would it make any sense if I said that I can't explain what I'm feeling?"

Monica leaned back in her chair and took a long sip of her drink. "Sarah, it would make more sense to admit that you don't understand what you're feeling."

Sarah reached out and grabbed her hand. "I do know one thing for sure," she said. "I'm a terrible friend."

"No, you're not," Monica said, squeezing her hand. "I'm the terrible friend. I should have told you about Marcus."

"Ok, fine. You're the terrible friend," Sarah replied with a grin. "How did you find him, by the way? Brooke?"

"Brooke," she replied.

"That little bitch," Sarah said with a smile. "I should never have told you about her or the store."

"Are you kidding? She's adorable."

"I know, as much as I hate to admit it."

Sarah looked over at the bar to see if she could tell how things were going based on the body language. Jack was as understanding as they come, but she was concerned this would have lasting effects. "Are we good?" Sarah finally asked. "I can only deal with one relationship crisis at a time, and no offense, but my marriage trumps our friendship."

"We are good, lady," Monica said as she stood up, helping Sarah to her feet.

Sarah hugged her. "Did you ever think we would be in a screwed-up situation like this?"

"Not in a million years."

Sarah held Monica's hand as they walked up to the bar where the boys were doing a shot. Jack turned as they approached. "Did you ladies work out your shit?" he asked.

"Yes," Sarah said. "Now we need to work out ours." Grabbing his hand, she pulled him back towards their table.

They were about to sit down when a slow song started playing. Still holding her hand, Jack guided her onto the dance floor and started dancing. Neither of them spoke for a while, just dancing in each other's arms.

"I'm sorry," Sarah finally said. "I honestly didn't mean to share anything with Monica. But you know she could tell something was going on between you and me, and she just kept digging. I thought sharing the one small sliver of what we have been doing would satisfy her."

Jack let out a long exhale as he continued to dance. "I think I am more concerned about your obvious feelings for Marcus. What was that all about?"

Sarah stopped dancing and led Jack back to their table. She sat down, holding his hands, and turned to face him. "I will do my best to explain something I don't fully understand. I love you with all my heart. And I had an amazing time that night with you and Marcus, as you know. It's a memory I enjoy going back to. Often. But for some reason, the thought of Monica being with him makes me think it will ruin my memories of that night. I don't love Marcus, but I do love those memories. Does that make any sense, or am I just rambling?"

Jack smiled and kissed her hand. "I suspect that there is more to it than that. But wherever our relationship goes from here, I will always be your husband, and he will always be your first who was not me," Jack said, squeezing her hand. "And, along those lines, CJ and Maddie as well."

A smile spread across Sarah's face. "That's quite an impressive group when you think about it, Jack."

"Yes, it is."

"Now, do you think we can salvage the rest of the night?"

"Yup. Right after you go apologize to Marcus."

CHAPTER TWENTY-EIGHT

Returning home from getting her hair done, Sarah found her sister, Ashley, seated on a stool at the island in her kitchen, reading a book. Next to Ashley was an enormous bouquet of roses.

"You're home early," Ashley said without looking up.

"I decided not to get my nails done," Sarah replied. "What are you doing here?"

"Reading," she said.

"No, I mean, why are you in my house?"

"I understand there has been some excitement in the William's household," Ashley said, ignoring her question.

"And what's with the roses?" Sarah asked, ignoring her comment.

"I don't know," Ashley replied. "You'll have to ask Viktor," she said, using a terrible Russian accent to stress his name. "Viktor with a K."

"You read the card?"

"Attached to more than a hundred roses? Of course. Have you met me?"

Sarah's heart skipped a beat as she pulled the card out of the envelope. It read:

"Sarah, I listened to you. When I got home, I did bad things with my wife. The roses are present from her. Blagodaryu ot vsey dushi. Viktor."

Sarah closed her eyes and lowered her head. "Did Mom read this?"

"You know she did," Ashley said. She closed the book as she stepped off the stool. She walked over and kissed Sarah on the side of the head. "I tried my best to stop her, but you know Mom."

"Fuck," Sarah said, resigned to the reality of the moment.

"I would say," Ashley said. "Now, who the hell is Viktor, and why is he sending you ten dozen long stem roses?"

"He is a Russian Oligarch who invested fifty million dollars with Jack's fund," she said.

"Holy shit," Ashley said.

"Drunk Sarah thought it would be a good idea to do some marriage counseling with him over an amazing five-course meal and a couple of bottles of vodka."

"And your advice was for him to go home and do bad things to his wife?"

"No, dammit, I told him to go home and do bad things with his wife."

"Oh," Ashley said. "Well, that clears things up."

"Wait," Sarah said as something clicked in her mind. "How did you know I came home early?" Sarah asked.

"It says on the printed schedule of events that you wouldn't be home until after four."

"What printed schedule?"

"The one Mom sent out with this book."

"What are you talking about?" Sarah said before she realized that Ashley was holding up the book's back cover for her to see. It took a second for Sarah's brain to process the skinny, pasty, worm of a man staring at her from the back cover, but there he was: Thomas L'Costa. "Are you saying what I think you're saying?"

"Oh yeah, we're going to have a big ol' intervention to save my little sister from herself and the evil doings of her awful husband."

"You have got to be freakin' kidding me," Sarah said as she grabbed the book out of Ashley's hand and threw it across the kitchen. "Ashley, can you please speak with Mom?"

"And exactly what would you like me to say?"

Sarah sat down on a stool. "What did she tell you?"

"You mean about your less than ladylike behavior?"

"You know exactly what I mean."

Ashley sat down on the stool next to Sarah and leaned against her, shoulder to shoulder. "She said that you and Jack have been going into the city a lot...."

"A lot, my ass. One night a month," Sarah blurted out.

"That you've been neglecting Colin."

"True, if you believe leaving him one night a month with her is neglect."

"And that she found some skimpy dress and a dildo."

"Good lord," Sarah said.

"And not just any dildo, apparently...."

"Enough."

"She wouldn't shut up about the dildo, Sarah. She kept talking to herself, repeating it over and over in different voices as if she was testing out which one sounded the best. Lifelike. Lifelike. Lifelike. Over and over."

"Thanks, Ashley. I get the picture."

Ashley put her arm across Sarah's shoulders. "All kidding aside, is there anything I should be concerned about?"

Sarah let out a deep exhale. "Ashley, other than the issues this has caused with Mom, Jack and I have never been happier."

"Ok, now answer one question for me."

"What's that?"

"What is the *this* you are talking about?"

Sarah let out a little laugh and squeezed Ashley's leg. "*This* is none of your business," she said.

Ashley walked across the room and picked the book up off the floor. "Promise me that I won't find a Jack and Sarah equivalent anywhere in these pages?"

"I promise," Sarah said.

Ashley walked back to the island and opened the book. "Fine. Then I need to get back to reading. I promised Mom I would finish it before the intervention."

Sarah shook her head. "Where is she?"

"I don't want to tell you," Ashley said quickly.

"Ashley, where is Mom?" she replied sternly.

"Come on, Sarah, I don't want to ruin the surprise."

"Ashley!" Sarah screamed. "Where the fuck is our mother?"

Ashley closed the book and placed it on the counter. Without looking up, she answered Sarah with as even a tone as possible. "She went to the train station to pick up Father Flanagan."

Sarah walked to the love seat in the bay window and sat down. Ashley watched as heavy breathing slowly turned into a tremble. It appeared that tears were soon to follow, but they never appeared. Sarah was past tears. Now she was just angry.

"Do you want me to get that?" Ashley asked.

Sarah looked up. "Get what?"

A moment later, the doorbell rang a second time. "Sorry, no. I'll get it." Walking to the front door, Sarah could see Monica through the window. "Why are you coming to the front door?" Sarah asked as she opened the door.

Monica held up a book with a black cover and blood-red writing.

"She invited you to my intervention? And you didn't tell me?" Sarah asked.

"Can I come in so we can talk?" Monica asked in an out-of-character meek voice.

Sarah stood to the side, holding the door open, but she said nothing.

"Thanks," Monica said as she walked past her and straight to the kitchen without stopping. "Hey, Ash," she said as she walked over to the dry bar and poured a glass of vodka. Reaching into the freezer, she grabbed a couple of ice cubes and leaned up against the island across from Ashley.

"Why didn't you at least warn me?" Sarah asked.

"Honestly, Sarah, your mom scares the crap out of me."

"Same," Ashley said without looking up from the book.

"She scares you? Really?" Sarah asked.

"I don't know, Sarah," Monica said as she took a large swallow of her drink. "She always has. I think it's a guilt thing, and I don't do guilt well."

"You don't do guilt well?" Sarah asked somewhat sarcastically.

"No, I don't," Monica said.

"Did you fuck Marcus?"

"Sarah, you know that's not fair," Monica said.

"What's not fair about it?"

"You said it was fine."

"No, Monica, I said I would give you his number if I had it."

"So, you are jealous?"

"No, of course not," Sarah said. "But, honestly..."

"Honestly, what?" Monica asked.

"Honestly, it pisses me off."

"Then why didn't you say that in the first place?"

"Because I am a married woman, and it isn't my place to

control who Marcus does or doesn't fuck just because he was the first man to go down on me since I got married."

Sarah heard a noise behind her but didn't move. Monica looked over Sarah's shoulder and then immediately at the ground. Sarah dropped her head and closed her eyes.

"Ahem," Sarah's mother said.

Sarah didn't say a word.

"Sarah, you remember Father Flanagan?"

CHAPTER TWENTY-NINE

Sarah couldn't bring herself to turn around and face him. "Yes, of course. Hello, Father."

"Hello, ladies. It's a pleasure to see you both after all these years. Though, I would prefer it be under different circumstances."

"Agreed," Sarah said, finally turning around to acknowledge the priest.

"I don't want to offend anyone, but when your mother asked me to be a part of an intervention, I thought for sure it would be for Ashley."

Ashely dropped the book flat on the island, making a large banging sound. "Don't you worry yourself, Padre. I have plenty of material for you to work with."

"Taking this opportunity for your confession would be a great joy," the priest said.

"Oh, I bet it would, Father," Ashley said. "But, there is that whole lead us not into temptation thing, right?"

The priest gave her a cold stare before turning to Maureen. "Could I trouble you into a cup of coffee?"

"Of course," Sarah and her mother said in unison.

Sarah stopped at Monica's side on her way to make some coffee. "I'm sorry," Sarah said in her ear. "I can be such a bitch."

"It's okay," Monica said, rubbing her arm.

As Sarah continued to make the coffee, the doorbell rang. "I'll get it," Maureen said. "That should be Thomas."

Sarah rolled her eyes and scooped out some ground coffee. Her mother called back from the front door. "Sarah, there's a young man named Ethan here that would like to speak with you."

Sarah froze. There had to be some explanation for why Ethan would, or even could, be at their door. It shouldn't be possible, but nothing seemed out of the question on a day like today. "Fuck me," she said under her breath.

Ashley hopped off her stool as Sarah turned and walked to the front door. "Something tells me I'm going to want to see this."

"Me, too," Monica said as she grabbed her vodka and fell in step behind the other girls.

"Mom, I've got this," Sarah said in as controlled a voice as she could muster. After her mother walked back into the kitchen, she glared at the other two women. "Can I have a little privacy, please?"

"Not a chance," Ashley said, pushing her a little to the side as she tried to look out the front door.

"Hi, Sarah."

"Ethan, what are you doing here?" Sarah asked, trying to keep the door as closed as possible. "How do you know where we live?"

"Your husband didn't clear the metadata off the pictures he sent me. A couple appear to have been taken at a hotel in the village, but the ones of you in the black lingerie and thigh-high stockings were taken here."

"Ok, Ethan, please stop talking."

Ashley and Monica listened from inside the hall, but this exchange was too much. They both pulled the door open at the same time.

"Sarah!" Ashley said as soon as she laid eyes on Ethan. "For the love of God, please tell me you aren't sleeping with this child?"

"No, it's nothing like that," Ethan said quickly.

Sarah let out a small sigh of relief that he had cleared that up before she had to.

"She wanted to have sex with my older brother. Not me."

"Ethan, what part of stop talking didn't you understand? This isn't appropriate. Go home."

"But it's my birthday," he said.

"Well, happy birthday, Ethan. Now, please go home," Sarah said.

"But I thought now that I am nineteen, things might be different."

Sarah took a deep breath. "Ethan, nothing is different. If you don't go home right now, I'll call your mother." She shooed the two women back into the house and closed the door.

"It's not what it seems," Sarah said, trying to reassure Ashley and Monica.

Ashley looked at Sarah like she had two heads. "Ok then, how old is the older brother? Thirty-two?"

"I'm not discussing this," she said as she walked back to the kitchen.

"Who was that, Sarah?" her mother asked.

"Just a boy from the neighborhood, Mom," Sarah replied. "Can I speak with you for a second? Alone?"

"Sure."

Sarah walked out the back door to the patio outside. She pulled out a chair and sat down. Her mother chose a seat across the table.

"Mom, what exactly do you think is going on between Jack and me?"

Her mother looked down at her hands as she sat there wringing them. "I think Jack is forcing you to do degrading, sexual acts that you would never be involved with if it weren't for him. That's what I think."

Sarah hoped to avoid a full disclosure discussion, but she couldn't allow her mother to feel that way about Jack for the rest of her life.

"Mom, if you want to have an intervention to save a manipulated spouse, Jack should be here because the intervention would be for him."

"What are you talking about?"

"All of this, Mom. Everything you suspect is going on is because of me."

Maureen scoffed. "Chapter Four, dear. How to Confront Denial."

"Mom, I'm not in denial."

"If you read the book, you would know that victims create fantastic alternate realities to justify their behavior."

"Mom, I put Jack in a position that he felt he had to choose between fulfilling my sexual fantasies or destroying our marriage."

"Sarah, would you listen to yourself? That makes no sense."

"But it's true, Mom."

"I will not have this. I want you to come inside and speak with Mr. L'Costa."

"Three men, Mom," Sarah said.

"What?"

"Tonight, Jack is helping me fulfill my fantasy of fucking three men at the same time."

"Jesus, Sarah. Why would you want to do such a thing? And why in the world would he allow it?"

"Because I fantasize about it, Mom. And because he loves me."

"A man doesn't do something like that because he loves you."

"Mom, he is afraid that if he doesn't, he will lose me."

"I don't believe you," Maureen said with tears running down her face.

"Mrs. Williams?" Ethan's voice came from the side of the yard.

Sarah turned in her chair so that she could see better. "I thought I asked you to go home, Ethan?"

"You did, but I spent all of my money getting here. Is there any way Yuri can give me another ride back to Jersey?"

"Sure, Ethan, under one condition."

"What's that?"

"Do you remember what you asked me when we were saying goodbye at the hotel in the village?"

"About the pictures of you?"

"Yes."

"I want you to tell my mother what I said you could do with them."

"You want me to tell your mother?"

"Yes, Ethan, I do."

"I'm not comfortable doing that," he said.

"Do you ever want me to send you more pictures?"

Ethan swallowed hard. "She said I can look at her pictures while I masturbate," he said, looking directly at Sarah's mother.

Sarah turned back to her mother and smiled.

"Thank you, Ethan. I will ask Yuri to pick you up out front."

"Thank you, Sarah," he replied.

"And Ethan?"

"Yes?"

"Happy birthday."

Ethan got a huge smile, nodded to the women, and skipped around the side of the house.

"How about now, Mom? You believe me now?" Sarah asked.

Maureen sat there with the same look on her face she had when she held Captain Lifelike in the living room.

"Sarah, that makes you a...."

"A lucky girl, Mom."

"A lucky girl?" Maureen asked in disbelief.

"Mom, I am the same daughter, mother, sister, and wife I was a year ago. Nothing about those relationships has changed."

"Sarah, you can't just run around satisfying your every urge like an animal."

"Mom, everything I have done, I have done with my husband."

"But how does this end, Sarah? How does this possibly end well?"

Sarah reached across the table and took her mother's hands in her own. "Mom, I don't know how it ends. What I do know is that a third of my married friends are already divorced, a third are currently cheating on each other, and the majority of the final third are just going through the motions. Jack and I? We are living out our fantasies with each other. So yes, I think it makes me a lucky girl."

Sarah sat back in her chair and looked out over the backyard. "Are you telling me that you and dad had amazing sex for thirty-five years?"

"Our sex life was fine," Maureen said dismissively.

"Was it everything you dreamed it would be? Did he make all of your fantasies come true?"

Maureen laughed. "Of course not, Sarah. It was marriage,

after all. But I loved your father. And our sex life was...." She paused as she struggled to find the right word.

"Adequate?" Sarah suggested.

"Yes. It was adequate."

Sarah smiled and let out a long, slow exhale. "Well, Mom, we aim for something more than adequate."

"You talk as if this is all normal."

"No, there is certainly nothing normal about it. But it does make us lucky. Different? Yes. But in my opinion? Lucky."

Maureen laughed as she wiped away her tears. "What am I going to tell Father Flanagan?"

"Oh, I'll handle Father Flanagan."

"No, you won't," Maureen said quickly. "I'll deal with him."

"Mom, I'll let you handle it, but you have to make me a promise?"

"What's that?"

"You need to be clear to anyone and everyone that you convinced that Jack was a cult leader...."

"I will, Sarah," Maureen chimed in. "I promise."

"Mom, if I hear so much as a whisper of something derogatory about Jack, I'll set them straight...with every little detail."

"I understand."

"Okay, then I'll give you a head start before I blow Father Flanagan's mind."

Maureen stood up and walked over to kiss the top of Sarah's head. "I don't know that I will ever fully understand this, but I promise to try. And I promise always to love you."

Sarah squeezed her mom's hand.

"Thanks, Mom. For the record, I've missed this. I've missed you."

"I've missed you, too, dear."

Maureen turned and walked back towards the house. Just before she reached the door, Sarah called out to her. "One more thing, Mom?"

"Sure."

"Can you please let Jack know that you don't hate him?"

"Well, I did, you know?"

"Yes, Mom, we both knew."

CHAPTER THIRTY

Sarah leaned back in her chair and stared at the sky. The days were getting shorter, and the sun lingered on the horizon. She had just realized how late it was when her phone rang.

"Hey," Jack said on the other end of the phone. "Are you close?"

"I haven't even left the house."

"Is everything okay?"

"Well, I don't have the energy to go through it all, so I'll give you the short version, okay?"

Jack laughed. "I'm honestly a little afraid right now."

"Well, here you go. I arrived home to find Ashley reading *The Unmaking of a Lady* at the island in our kitchen."

"What was Ashley doing there?"

"Jack, if you interrupt me with questions after every point, it will take all night."

"Okay, sorry. Please continue."

"So, Ashley is in our kitchen reading that book because she promised Mom she would have it read before the intervention."

"Intervention?"

"Jack, please."

"Sorry, continue."

"She promised to have it read before the intervention to free me from your clutches. In addition to Ashley, Mom invited Monica, of all people...don't say a word, Jack...Also we have Father Flanagan, our childhood priest, and none other than the Cult Leader Whisperer himself, Thomas L'Costa." She paused to take a deep breath. "On top of all of this, Ethan showed up at our front door—not a word, Jack—proposing that his birthday—that was today—should be sufficient for me to reconsider sleeping with him."

"Please tell me that is everything?"

"No, Jack, there was a bouquet of roses the size of Grand Central Station delivered to the house with a note from a crazy, billionaire Russian thanking me for the advice to do bad things to his wife."

"With his wife."

"Yes, with his wife."

There was a long silence before Jack continued. "Is that everything?"

Sarah laughed. "I told Mom the truth."

"The whole truth?"

"Enough of it that you are her favorite son-in-law again."

"I'm sorry. I can't imagine that was an easy conversation."

"Nope. But it was the only way to derail the nonsense out here and restore your good name."

"I don't care about my good name," Jack said.

Sarah genuinely loved this man. "I know you don't, babe. But it is important to me."

"Are you back to being the favorite daughter?"

"Oh, no," she laughed. "That ship has sailed."

"I'm sorry. Maybe in time."

"Maybe," she said. "At least she can look me in the eye again without the Captain Lifelike stare."

"Baby steps," Jack said. "Are you headed this way, or are we pulling the plug on the evening? As it turns out, a couple of people down here are looking forward to spending time with you tonight."

"Oh no, I just need to kick a priest and his helper to the curb, and I'll be on my way...though Yuri is halfway to Jersey now."

"Ethan?"

"Ethan."

"How did he find out where we live?"

"That's a part of the long story I will tell you later."

"Are you waiting on Yuri or finding another way down here?"

"Depends on how long it takes me to kick everyone out of our house," Sarah said. "I'll send you an ETA once I'm en route."

"Looking forward to it."

"Ditto."

Sarah hung up the phone and turned around to look in the kitchen window. Thomas L'Costa had arrived, and it appeared he was arguing with her mother. Walking in the back door, it went from four people talking over each other to complete silence instantly.

"Oh, please, don't stop on my behalf," Sarah said.

Mr. L'Costa stepped forward and offered Sarah his hand. "Hello, Ms. Williams. I am Thomas L'Costa."

"Mrs. Williams," Sarah replied.

"Yes, of course. Mrs. Williams."

Maureen quickly chimed in. "Sarah, I've tried to explain that this has all been a big misunderstanding."

"Maureen, you need to trust the process," Thomas L'Costa

said. "Denial is always the first response to these situations, from the abuser to the abused to the family closest to them."

"Hey, does anyone here want to know a secret?" Ashley chimed in. "I mean, chapter twelve in your book talks about how lies damage the very fabric of any relationship."

"Yes, Ashley, the truth is always best," L'Costa said in a loving, reassuring tone. "Thank you so much for being brave and willing to share."

"Okay," Ashley said. "Here goes. You see the priest over there, Father Flanagan? He likes to dress in women's clothes."

Father Flanagan grabbed onto the island with both hands as his legs almost collapsed beneath him. "Ashley, that is not true. How could you say such a thing?"

"So, you deny it?" Ashley asked.

"On everything that is holy," the priest said.

"I wouldn't be so certain, everyone," Ashley replied. "Chapter three, Denial Always Comes First."

"Ashley," Maureen said. "How could you accuse the priest of such a thing? Have you lost your mind?"

"No, Mom. I just couldn't go through life being the favorite daughter," Ashley said as she winked at Sarah. "Besides, you've tried to get the pseudo-shrink to leave your house for twenty minutes. I just thought this might help the cause."

"Go ahead and leave your sister in some man's clutches, for all I care. But you don't have to ask me twice to leave," L'Costa said as he grabbed his briefcase and stormed down the hall, headed for the front door.

"What are you talking about," Ashley yelled after him. "She's asked you to leave like four or five times?"

There was a loud slam of the front door.

"Sorry, Father," Ashley said. "I was just trying to make a point."

"In the future, Ashley, please leave my reputation out of

any future efforts to help if you would be so kind," the priest asked politely.

"You got it, Padre. Now, I'm about to drive my little sister into the city to see her wonderful husband. You want me to drop you off along the way?"

"I will accept your generous offer under two conditions."

"Ok, what you got?" Ashley asked.

"That you promise to drive the speed limit and that we discuss happy memories of your childhood while we ride. And nothing else."

"It's a deal."

"You don't mind?" Sarah asked.

"Not at all. Besides, there are a few details I will need you to fill in for me," she said with a smile.

"Once you drop me off," the priest insisted.

"A deal's a deal, Padre. Nothing but happy memories for you until you get out of the car and then...."

"Yes, fine, happy childhood memories," the priest confirmed.

Turning to walk upstairs, Sarah grabbed Monica's hand. "Come with me," Sarah said. Sarah sat on the bed and patted the space next to her when they got to her bedroom. Monica gave her a funny look before taking a seat next to her.

"Do you know what I plan to do tonight? And more importantly, do you know who I plan to do it with?"

"I do."

"And you're okay with it?"

"I am now," Monica said.

"What do you mean?"

"Marcus told me that Jack had asked if he wanted to help with tonight's gathering."

"And?"

"Marcus said he needed to know that I was okay with it."

"You two have become that close?"

"We have."

"Then he shouldn't be a part of this evening," Sarah said, disappointed.

"Oh, I disagree. Marcus wasn't lying when he said that he had a high libido. He's the first man I can't keep up with in bed."

"So, are you really okay with it?"

"Sweetie, I would much rather have fifty percent of amazing than one hundred percent of nothing." She leaned over and kissed her on the cheek. "Besides, one day, I might need help fulfilling a fantasy of my own," she said with a grin.

"With Jack?" Sarah asked, wide-eyed.

"Maybe," Monica said, kissing her hand. "Or maybe with his wife."

Sarah leaned back and turned to face her. "Oh my, Monica Parker. Is there something you need to tell me?"

CHAPTER THIRTY-ONE

As Ashley pulled up to the curb in front of the Aspect East Village Hotel, Sarah reached over and grabbed her hand. Sarah searched for the right words to thank her. She also wanted to find the right words to explain everything. In the end, the best she could do was smile as a single tear rolled down her face.

Ashely looked up and returned the smile. "Anytime, baby sister. Anytime."

Sarah nodded, composed herself, and stepped out to the curb.

"Hey," Ashely yelled right before Sarah closed the door. "Do you love Jack?"

"With all my heart," she said.

"Does he love you?"

Sarah laughed. "Adores the ground I walk on."

"Then fuck everyone else," Ashley said with a quick shrug and a smile. "Why do you care what other people think?"

Sarah gently shook her head, smiled, and gave Ashley a single wave of her hand goodbye.

"See ya," Ashley said as she pulled away.

Sarah's thoughts were racing as she walked into the hotel lobby. She knew the boys were waiting on her upstairs, but she wanted to spend a minute alone to gather her thoughts. She took a seat at the bar and ordered vodka and soda. The events over the past year had been pretty significant. Her relationship with Jack was stronger now than ever, but bringing other people into their bedroom certainly posed risks that didn't exist a year ago. But was there any safety in trying to live for fifty years with an adequate monogamous sex life? Did they need to include others to find that level of excitement, or were they just being lazy? Sarah couldn't answer any of those questions. The truth was, only time would tell. But at the moment, she was happy with where the odd series of events had brought them.

Her cell phone rang.

"Hey, Jack," she said into her phone.

"Hey, where are you? I thought you would be here by now?" he said.

"Are you missing your girlfriend?" she asked playfully.

"Oh, thank God," Jack said. "For a moment there, I thought my wife had answered the phone."

"Well, truth be told, she was here a minute ago, but I sent her on her way."

"Whew," Jack said. "That sounds like a close one. Now, where is here?"

"Downstairs at the hotel bar."

"I thought we agreed to meet up here, but I can wrangle the troops and head downstairs if you prefer."

"No, I just needed a minute alone."

"You okay?"

"Yes, everything is great."

"You sure?"

"Positive. Let me pay the tab, and I'll head that way."

Sarah laughed to herself as she looked around the bar.

Three or four different couples were sitting around the bar, all staring at their smartphones—or staring at their date who was staring at their smartphone. What was it that they got out of being glued to the devices? Sarah didn't need to look for any stimulation on her phone. She had plenty of it waiting for her upstairs.

Jack greeted her at the hotel suite with a hug and a gentle kiss. "Sorry you had to go through that," he said.

"It's fine. I have a feeling we are good."

"You think your mom can really understand and accept this part of our lives?"

"I think there is a pretty good chance. We'll know more tomorrow."

Jack looked at her with a cocked head. "What will we know tomorrow?"

"If she understands that adequate is no way to live," she said with a grin.

Jack took a step back from her and looked her in the eye. "What did you do?"

"Nothing."

"Seriously, what did you do?"

"I may or may not have left Captain Lifelike in a bag by her bed," Sarah said with a giggle.

"You didn't?"

"Oh, I did," she said. "And I left a note with it."

Jack walked and sat down on the couch in the living room and put his head in his hands. "I'm so afraid to ask…."

Sarah followed him into the living room, straddled him on the couch, and kissed him. "The note simply said: Adequate sucks, Mom. Try life on the edge."

"You didn't?"

"I did," she said, kissing him again. "I even signed it. Love, Sarah."

Jack groaned. "I will never be able to look her in the eye again."

"Well, if it is gone when we get home, we'll have our answer." Looking up at Marcus and CJ, who were both quietly standing off to the side, she said, "Hello, boys." Climbing off Jack, she walked over and gave each a passionate kiss. "I see my room service hasn't arrived."

"We had some champagne delivered earlier, but nothing else has arrived. I would call down for you, but...I can't have my employees know I'm cavorting with guests," CJ said with a laugh.

As if on cue, there was a knock on the door.

"Jack, can you grab that, please?" Sarah asked as she grabbed Marcus and CJ by the hand and led them to the bedroom. "I ordered something special. Off menu," Sarah said. "And Jack, I ordered this for you."

None of them could see the door to the suite open from the bedroom, but they could hear the silence that followed.

"If I made a mistake, you are welcome to send it back," Sarah yelled into the next room. "But I think you should try it at least once. If you don't like it, I promise not to force it on you ever again."

There was a long silence. "Jack?" Sarah called out.

"Are you sure about this?" Jack yelled back.

"Yes, I'm sure."

A moment later, Jack walked into the bedroom with Brooke holding his hand.

"Are you sure you know what you're doing?" Jack asked.

Sarah walked over to Brooke and passionately kissed her.

"Damn," Brooke said when she finally came up for air. "I knew you were one hot momma."

Sarah grabbed Jack's hand and guided him onto his back in the middle of the bed. Brooke immediately climbed up on the other side of Jack and began to help Sarah undress him.

"Are you sure you're okay with this?" he asked Sarah one more time.

"Yes, Jack. I wouldn't have gone to all the trouble to arrange this if I wasn't sure."

Making eye contact with Jack, Brooke smiled as she unbuttoned the last button on his shirt and threw it open wide.

"And you're sure you're ok with this?" Jack asked, looking at Brooke.

Brooke unbuckled his belt. "Of course. I think it's an honor to be your first."

Sarah noticed CJ and Marcus standing off to the side, staring like a couple of excited schoolboys watching their first porn. "Don't you worry, boys. Your time is coming," she said with a grin. "You're welcome to watch, but not from the bed. You'll need to bring your own chairs."

Sarah slid down to the foot of the bed, racing to get Jack's shoes and socks off before Brooke had his pants undone. For CJ and Marcus, the ladies looked like a NASCAR pit crew racing the clock. Once Jack was naked, Sarah crawled up by his side and pulled a box of condoms out of the nightstand drawer. Brooke worked her way to the other side of Jack and gently began to rub his erection.

Sarah leaned in and whispered in Jack's ear. "Do you want me to hold your hand?"

Jack squeezed her hand and turned to face her. "Sarah. Here. Now," he saith a smile before leaning in to kiss her.

Sarah made eye contact with Brooke as she hesitated over Jack's cock. Brooke smiled and asked, "Are we sticking with the plan?"

"We are," Sarah replied.

"You sure?" Brooke asked as she began to quicken the pace she was stroking Jack.

"I am," Sarah said with a wink. "Geronimo."

Brooke got a huge smile and dropped her mouth around Jack's cock.

"Holy mother of God," Jack said.

Sarah pinched Jack's nipple as she watched Brooke give a mesmerizing combination of handjob and blowjob. "Why Jack, I don't think I have ever seen you this hard," Sarah said in a tone making fun of all the times he was surprised about how wet Sarah would get with other men.

Brooke twisted her hand around his cock while driving her mouth down over it. And then she would turn her hand back the other way as she pulled her head back up.

"Brooke, I'd be careful," CJ said from the sidelines with a small laugh.

"No, it's too late," Jack said. "Please don't stop. I'm begging you. Please don't stop."

Sarah leaned over Jack and planted a deep passionate kiss on him. Jack let out a long guttural moan as he came in Brooke's mouth.

"Jack," Sarah said with a playful voice. "You stupido?"

"I don't care who you are," CJ said from his chair by the bed. "Nothing stupido about that."

Jack remained sprawled out on his back, trying to catch his breath. Sarah leaned over and kissed him.

"Thank you," he said, panting.

"Don't thank me. Thank Brooke," Sarah said with a smile.

"I thank you both."

The hours that followed far exceeded Sarah's expectations. Brooke added an element to the evening that wasn't present in her original fantasy. The strange joy Sarah got from watching Brooke pleasure Jack surprised her. She didn't tell Jack, but the wettest she had ever been was when she watched Jack make love with Brooke.

By the time the evening came to an end, they were out of

champagne, out of condoms, and out of combinations of partners.

"This bed is a wreck," Jack said once all of their guests had left. "Do you want to get some clean sheets brought up? Or at least make the bed?"

"Nope," Sarah said. "I'm good right here." She placed her head on Jack's chest.

Jack rubbed her hair. "Did you want to make love with your boyfriend?"

Sarah lifted her head and gave him a dirty look. "Are you kidding me?"

Jack shrugged his shoulders and smiled. "I thought I would try."

She laid her head back on his chest and closed her eyes. "If you are good, maybe your wife will give you a little missionary in the morning."

"That sounds adequate," Jack said, being a smart-ass.

"No, Jack," Sarah said, drifting off to sleep. "That sounds perfect."

THE END

ABOUT THE AUTHOR

Who is Denice Holt?

Good question. I'm a writer, mother, partner, lover, and wife. Whew! I love to cook. I'm a sucker for Kir Royales. And I am blessed to enjoy the company of a good man and three precocious boys. I keep a watchful eye on the future, but I strive to enjoy the little moments in life as they go by every day.

Though I'm still a small-town girl at heart, I have lived a reasonably big-city life. I've learned a lot of things along the way that I should know...and a few that I probably shouldn't.

Advice for young parents? Hug and kiss your kids every chance you get because you will blink and they will think it's gross.

Advice for young couples? Don't let the distractions of life —kids, work, money—cause you to lose who you are as a couple. Date through it all! If you were ever madly in love, you could be again.

Advice for young lovers? Don't be afraid to venture out on the ledge a bit. It will make you sad to find out when you're eighty that nipple clamps were your jam all along. ☺

Oh yeah, and then there is my writing. I love relationships. I love happy relationships. I also happen to love sex. So, I write what I love. If you come along for the ride, I promise you this: everything I write ends with a happy-ever-after, a happy-for-now, or, some of my favorites, a happy-for-the-memories.

Discover other books by Denice Holt at:

www.DeniceHolt.com

3.35.14.0

Made in United States
Orlando, FL
13 July 2023